SEX AS A SECOND LANGUAGE

Jamie Sobrato

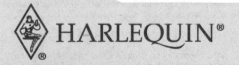

TORONTO • NEW YORK • LONDON
AMSTERDAM • PARIS • SYDNEY • HAMBURG
STOCKHOLM • ATHENS • TOKYO • MILAN • MADRID
PRAGUE • WARSAW • BUDAPEST • AUCKLAND

ISBN-13: 978-0-373-79320-4
ISBN-10: 0-373-79320-0

SEX AS A SECOND LANGUAGE

ABOUT THE AUTHOR

Jamie Sobrato lived in and traveled around Europe for five years and suspects that sex is indeed the unofficial language of the city of Rome, the setting for *Sex as a Second Language*. Now she lives in Northern California, where she writes for the Harlequin Blaze line and hopes to someday soon break out her Lonely Planet travel guides again and head back to Italy.

Books by Jamie Sobrato

HARLEQUIN BLAZE

84—PLEASURE FOR PLEASURE
116—WHAT A GIRL WANTS
133—SOME KIND OF SEXY
167—AS HOT AS IT GETS
190—SEXY ALL OVER
216—ANY WAY YOU WANT ME
237—ONCE UPON A SEDUCTION*
266—THE SEX QUOTIENT*
284—A WHISPER OF WANTING†

HARLEQUIN TEMPTATION

911—SOME LIKE IT SIZZLING
997—TOO WILD

*It's All About Attitude
†Lust Potion #9

To the Naked Page people, for hanging out on my blog and listening to me whine incessantly

1

http://sexasasecondlanguage.blogworld.com
Sex As a Second Language—A blog about the
erotic exploits of an American girl in Europe.

Could You Please Shave That?
(Or why I had to get the hell out of Greece faster
than the speed of the local train service)

He had the firm, sinewy thighs of a soccer player and the darkly expressive eyes of a man with
a deep longing. I had to know—was he longing
for his next drink of ouzo, for Greece to win the
World Cup or for me?

And I should have known better. Having just
broken up with my boyfriend, I was on the rebound, and rebound judgment is notably flawed.
Plus, perfect lovers never fall into my lap the way
he did. I mean, he *literally* fell into my lap one
night at the rowdy bar where he worked.

No, in the real world, great lovers need to be
carefully sought out, tested, cultivated. Extremely

rare is the man who knows all the right moves on the first encounter.

And there is no worse surprise than discovering that the man you are about to get down and dirty with has a hairy ass. Not just a little hair, either. We're talking a full-on coat of fur covering the ass cheeks. I've never seen anything like it, and I hope like crazy I never do again.

I just didn't know how to get past that. My first thought was to feign violent stomach cramps and get the hell out before I burst into laughter, but he was so earnest, so eager, so…erect. It would have been beyond cruel to bolt that far into the game.

So I'd have to avoid touching or looking at his ass. Not too big a deal, right? Well…he had mirrors over his bed.

And while normally that might add a fun extra dimension to our sexual exploits, this time, it was like watching a documentary on gorilla sex. Maybe that's not the most inspired description, but I am, truly, at a loss for words here. And we all know how rarely that happens. Let's just say a change of position was in order, so that I didn't have to stare at the mirrored ceiling any longer than necessary.

I'll spare you the gruesome details. I only mention this to show you why I had to leave Greece, a country where I spent nearly one year and had six lovers, all of whom were far too hairy.

Comments:
1. Juno says: *Ewwww.* Butt cheek hair!

2. Mariana says: You poor girl. I hope Italy proves more fun for you.

3. calidude says: Can u post pics?

4. Eurogirl says: No, sorry, no pics allowed. Must protect the innocent and hairy. And besides, this was one instance where I definitely had no desire for a camera in the bedroom.

5. Anonymous says: I know why you really left Greece, and it had nothing to do with that guy.

Rome, Italy

THE GUY THREE TABLES OVER was hot. Seriously hot. But Ariel Turner, world-traveling connoisseur of men, could not catch his eye. Even more frightening, she was having a hard time even working up the desire to flirt.

Had the whole world gone to hell, or just her life?

Ariel, known to the blogosphere as Eurogirl, loved three things—sex, caffeine and the written word. But sometimes sex could get a girl into serious trouble, as could the written word. So now her only safe vice seemed to be caffeine, and the whole situation was making her cranky. Not to mention the gorgeous guy in Armani reading the paper and ignoring her.

She turned her gaze from the guy across the café back to her laptop computer. Her stomach balled up as she read the fifth comment on her blog. Who the hell had written it? Did anyone really know why she'd left Greece? And if so, how had they found out her blogging identity? She was seriously screwed if so.

She deleted the fifth comment, then closed the Comments window, inhaled the heavy scent of pollution in the air and took another sip of her latte in a doomed attempt to calm her nerves. Around her, the city bustled with foot traffic through the piazza and past the outdoor café that had already become her favorite spot to write when the May heat was unbearable inside her one-room apartment.

Normally by now, she would have had fifty or sixty responses to her post, but Sex As a Second Language was dead in the water at the moment. Maybe it had been that creepy fifth comment, or maybe she just sucked. She needed to write a new entry, for sure. Her most recent one was lame at best, a lie she'd concocted to cover up the truth about her Greece disaster and subsequent flight from the country.

She gazed over at the hot guy again, forcing herself to admire the way his suit perfectly hugged his wide shoulders, the way his lips sensuously hugged his cigarette…. But she wasn't feeling it. She continued to stare, thinking maybe if she caught his eye and he began to flirt, she'd get her groove back and join in the festivities.

But when he finally glanced up and his gaze glossed over her as if she was wallpaper, she felt her hopes wane even more. He wasn't wearing a wedding ring, and her impeccable gaydar had labeled him firmly heterosexual. So maybe it was her. Maybe she was sending out bad vibes.

No surprise there. It was no wonder she didn't feel like writing lately. Changing jobs and countries always threw her off her creative stride a bit. Factor in the extra stress of the past month—family drama, relationship drama and general angst about life— and she had the perfect formula for a mild case of depression and a raging case of writer's block.

How could she have known that Kostas, the svelte, loose-hipped bartender with the agile hands—and for the record, a perfectly nice, nonhairy ass—was, in actuality, a terrorist?

He'd been her lover for five months before she'd become suspicious of his mysterious comings and goings from her life. She had begun to wonder if he was married—one sexual boundary Eurogirl had no desire to cross.

After Kostas had borrowed her laptop a few times, Ariel had seen the opportunity to snoop on his activities. Being a traveling blogger, she'd acquired enough computer expertise to know that nothing was really deleted from a hard drive. She was able to use a device in her software meant to protect against accidental deletion to retrieve his Internet history.

It had only taken a quick glimpse to reveal his deep interest in the November 17 movement, a radical group who garnered both public sympathy and scorn, depending on one's political leanings.

Needing her curiosity confirmed, she had taken a peek into his e-mail and discovered that he was not only actively involved in the movement, but was also fearful that he was being watched by the government.

Having suffered through 9/11, terrified for her little brother—who at the time had worked in the twin towers of the World Trade Center—Ariel's stomach contracted at the mere word *terrorist*. And she was even more horrified when she thought of how many times she had accepted a package or seemingly innocent message for Kostas from one of the names on his e-mail list. Had she aided a terrorist?

Ariel's first thought had been to call the police, but she realized there was a good chance she'd end up in a foreign jail. So she'd bolted the next morning, stopping at a public pay phone to make an anonymous call about Kostas to the police. Then she'd boarded the first train to the airport and headed for Rome.

"*Bellisima!*"

Ariel glanced up from her laptop computer and smiled at the passing man who was still grinning at her, still staring as if she were sitting at the café stark naked. Only her fifth day in Italy, and she was already growing accustomed to the outrageous flirtatiousness of Roman men. Too bad that one looked about as appealing as her great-uncle Stan, but still. This was progress.

For the first time in her life, Ariel was having trouble working up the enthusiasm to find a new guy. This was bad, especially for a writer of erotic memoirs—and a blogger in need of current material. She'd always drifted happily from one guy to the next, and she'd assumed that's how she'd always be, but now…

It had to be the stress, the upheaval, the depression. Depression. Ugh. Such a downer concept.

She'd never considered herself one of *those* people before. And yet here she was, thirty years old, the world at her fingertips, in her favorite city, but she wasn't happy. She finally had to face that her dearth of energy and creativity was something bigger than a bad mood.

But Ariel believed sitting around feeling sorry for herself was not the way to live her life. She had to be proactive. She had to plow forward, shitty feelings be damned.

Her gaze landed again on the man she'd seen for three days in a row at the café. He had all the important surface ingredients. He was tall, gorgeous, well-dressed and…leaving the café, damn it. He talked on his mobile phone as he passed by. At any other time in her life, he would have been a guy she'd strike up a conversation with. The old Ariel would have been flirting with him like mad. The old Ariel would have at least been able to catch his eye.

So what had changed?

She closed her laptop, jammed it into its carrying case, downed the last of her latte and hurried after him. Maybe she couldn't work up the nerve to full-on flirt, but she could do something.

She could follow him.

Two days later...

MARC SORRELLA watched the bank of surveillance monitors and tried to keep his eyes open in spite of the relentless dullness of the job. He was trying to be Zen about the whole thing, his mind and spirit at rest and calm in the face of such a boring task.

Zen? Who the hell was he kidding? He may have enjoyed reading the work of the great Buddhist philosophers, but he was an utter and complete failure at achieving a state that even remotely resembled placid. He needed another espresso. Like right now. He glanced at his watch and saw that it was only a little after ten—if he went for more coffee, he'd be too wired to form another coherent thought for the rest of the day.

Filling in for the morning surveillance guy at the U. S. Embassy was dull work, but it afforded Marc a chance to watch the comings and goings in and around the building from the vantage point of every security camera, and for a CIA agent, that was occasionally invaluable.

As a clandestine operative, he worked at the embassy under the guise of being a security guard, but what he actually did was watch and listen for potential threats to national safety. He kept his eyes and ears open at all times, always aware, always hyperalert.

His current mission at the embassy was to investigate a possible plot by a local terrorist cell to launch coordinated attacks on American-Embassy personnel. So far, all he'd managed to do was defuse a couple of bomb scares and assure everyone that a schizophrenic man who'd gotten into the building and started yelling and causing a commotion was not actually a threat to anyone but himself.

A willowy form entered one of the video screens, and Marc's gaze followed it to the fountain's edge. Strappy sandals, long, lean legs, a black sundress, lush lips, dark sunglasses, long brown hair. Stunning.

And familiar to him.

But from where? He hadn't dated her, hadn't run into her here at work, but…but he'd seen her in that exact spot before, maybe even on video footage.

Perhaps. He stared at her for a while, and his cock stirred in his pants. Damn it. He couldn't sit here watching for terrorists with a boner.

He spun around at his desk and flipped on an unused monitor, navigated through the computer menu of footage to the day before and rewound until he found what he was looking for. Same woman, nearly same time of day, sitting in front of the embassy on the edge of the fountain.

He rewound further, to two days prior, and found the woman again in the saved footage.

What was she doing? And why?

"Find something good there, Marco?" Florio Devoti asked in his Napoli-tinged Italian.

"*Si,*" Marc muttered. He was known to everyone in his Italian life as Marco Antonetti. That was his assumed identity—Marco the security guard. No one could know his real name, Marc Anthony Sorrella, or that he was American and knew fifteen different ways to kill a man with his bare hands.

Florio was the head security guard on the day shift, but he spent most of his time scoping out women and jerking off to porn in the men's restroom. He leaned over Marc's shoulder and expelled an appreciative whistle when he laid eyes on the mystery woman. Dear God, Marc wasn't about to become another Florio. His erection went flaccid instantly.

"Three days in a row she's been in front of the embassy," Marc said.

"Back that up again," Florio said. "I want a better view of her ass."

Marc hit the rewind button, and they watched the footage again.

"Look there—she's watching Lucci, don't you think?" Florio said, making a useful observation for once.

Giovanni Lucci, to be more specific, the controversial political figure who had gotten a share of media attention in recent months thanks to his extremist views.

Marc forwarded the footage to the previous day,

and yes, the woman was watching Lucci walk by. So she was watching him daily, which made her someone Marc needed to be watching. Not that he truly gave a damn about the near-fascist politician's fate, but given that the man was currently working at the embassy, Marc had to care. Any potential terrorist threat had to be taken seriously.

And when the potential threat was so easy on the eyes, it wasn't much of a chore. He turned his attention to the monitors showing real time and found the woman still sitting in the same spot. Just sitting. And watching. Either she was a really bad spy, or she had too much time on her hands.

And what was she carrying in her laptop bag? A computer, or a makeshift bomb?

"I forgot to tell you, your girlfriend showed up today, and I had the pleasure of escorting her out," Florio said.

Marc glanced up and caught his smirk. "You must mean *ex*-girlfriend."

"The one with the big tits."

Marc winced inwardly at the description but knew it would do no good to correct Florio. He'd always gone to great pains to keep his work life separate from his personal life, and this was a reminder of what a bad idea it was not to follow that rule.

"Did she cause a scene?"

Florio smiled. "Only a small one."

"What happened?"

"She came to the reception desk and demanded

to see you, said you were waiting to see her, and when I interceded, she did a bit of kicking and screaming on the way out."

"Shit. I'm surprised I didn't hear about this sooner."

"It happened first thing, seven o'clock. I've been busy since or I would have tracked you down."

"Thanks, man."

"I'll catch you later," Florio said as he left.

Marc pulled his mobile phone out of his pocket and turned it on—he normally kept it off on the job—and sure enough, there were three text messages waiting for him from Lucia.

Message # 1: Bastard

Message # 2: How could u ditch me like that?

Message # 3: I thought u were different.

They hadn't seen each other for a month until last night when he'd accidentally bumped into Lucia in a bar, while chatting up another woman, no less. She'd gotten pissed, and he had to admit, rightly so. When he saw himself through her eyes, there wasn't much denying that he was a bastard....

A serial dater. He hadn't heard the term before Lucia had thrown it at him in a voice mail when he'd broken up with her by avoiding her calls.

Serial dater—as in, the kind of guy who went

through woman after woman, dumping them without warning. He'd gotten so used to not getting emotionally close to people in his work, he'd turned it into a pattern in his whole life.

Marc closed the phone and put it back in his pocket. Nothing he could say to her messages, really. They were true.

He'd created his own problems. When the Buddhist monks wrote about Right Action, Marc always squirmed. In all the ways he was a failure at the whole Buddhism thing, that one rang truest of all. His actions, when it came to women, were anything but conscionable.

He turned his attention back to the woman still sitting on the fountain. He used the photo capture function on the video screen, zoomed in on the woman's face, saved it as a JPEG and brought up the CIA database screen. Two minutes later, a photo-matching search gave him her name, Ariel Turner, and known history as a terrorist consort in Greece, along with her secret history as an anonymous sex blogger known as Eurogirl.

Terrorist consort? Anonymous sex blogger? First interesting thing Marc had come across all month.

Definitely worth investigating further.

2

Worst. Sex. Ever.

Call it bad karma, call it bad luck—call it whatever you want. I'll just call it bad. Maybe I was trying to get my stride back after the hairy-assed Greek, and made another misstep, but the sad truth is that you have to sleep with a lot of frogs to finally find your bedroom prince. And apparently I am all about amphibian sex lately.

I met him on the subway. He sat down next to me and started playing a strange sort of flute I'd never seen before. My first instinct was to get up and move, but then I noticed how deftly his fingers moved over the instrument, and how nice those fingers were (and we all know by now what a weakness I have for good hands), and before I knew it I was making eye contact, admiring his five o'clock shadow and asking him his name.

An hour later, we were back at my place and there was a copy of Kafka's *Metamorphosis* wedged under my left shoulder blade, discarded this morning on the bed before I suspected

I'd be bringing a flutist home for some non-musical fun.

"That's it—don't stop! Don't stop!"

All I'd done was kiss his ear.

I frowned at the guy's neck and tried not to laugh. I nipped at his earlobe, and got the same wildly enthusiastic response a second time. Like he was about to come.

"You've got sensitive ears," I whispered. "Is the rest of you so responsive?"

"Oh, yeah," he groaned as I eased my hand down his belly to his erection.

I gripped it lightly, and he expelled a startled gasp, doubled over and convulsed. Come shot across his belly, all over my hand—you get the idea. I tried not to show my disappointment, but it wasn't like he couldn't guess.

Language barriers and musical talents aside, it's pretty much universally understood that premature ejaculation isn't exactly the way to a girl's heart.

AND THAT WAS, OFFICIALLY, the dumbest blog entry Ariel had ever drafted. Not to mention that it was mostly lies. Well, the incident was real, but it hadn't happened recently, and it hadn't happened here in Rome. She'd once been with a prematurely ejaculating flutist, and she'd once had Kafka wedged under her shoulder during sex, but she hadn't been with anyone since her Greek disaster.

What was a newly celibate sex blogger supposed to blog about? Not having sex?

She clicked the Save to Drafts button and filed the entry away, where it would likely never see the light of day. Another morning at the café, another day without anything interesting to write, another day to contemplate her uselessness in the universe.

She was full of cheery thoughts. It turned out that when she wasn't frenetically running around screwing every guy who turned her on, she had time to contemplate how sad it was that she needed validation so badly, and from so many men. And to consider how she'd abandoned her brother to move to Europe when he had barely gotten back on his feet after coming out of a twelve-step program.

She gazed over at her mystery guy again, watched him reading his usual morning paper and sipping his usual morning coffee, and decided she had become truly pathetic hanging out here and following him every day.

To make matters worse, the family she'd interviewed with for the tutoring job had not called back. All in all, Rome was sucking the big one.

Her life had veered into pointlessness, and without her writing to sustain her, it was becoming more apparent by the day. Writing was the one way she had to feel good about herself anymore. It was her way of connecting to people, entertaining them, and without it she had, basically, nothing. Actually, she had nothing on a deadline.

Six months ago, a literary agent who read Sex As a Second Language had contacted Ariel saying she loved the blog and wanted to know if she'd be interested in turning the content into a book of memoirs. That had been Ariel's dream from the start, but she'd gotten a little sidetracked by having fun and living her life. The book idea had always been something she figured she'd do later, once she had a bit of perspective about things. Or something like that.

A month after she'd first heard from her agent, Lucinda Martinez, Ariel had an impressive book deal before the book had even been written. At times throughout the past few years, her blog had been one of the hottest on the Internet, her publishers banking on that popularity to generate sales.

Her assigned editor seemed convinced that completing the book would simply be a matter of compiling her entries and polishing them up a bit, but Ariel knew there was more to it than that. For one thing, she didn't have a logical conclusion to her erotic adventures. There wasn't any overarching theme, no cohesiveness, no tidy ending—just a bunch of sexual essays.

All she had was a deadline to get the completed book to her editor by the end of the year and a dwindling advance check. Rome was an expensive city, after all. Which gave added weight to her time in Italy. She needed to make it mean something. And she needed to do it before she went broke.

She closed her laptop and stowed it in its bag

again, as she watched the mystery guy stand to leave. Yes, despite the lecture she had just given herself, she was going to follow him again, and no, she didn't feel any closer to working up the nerve to approach him. Rather, she'd just gotten so out of touch with reality that following him was part of her pointless daily routine. What the hell else did she have to do?

As she walked behind him at a safe distance, her mobile phone rang, and she saw from the LCD that it was her little brother, Trey, calling. Only days ago, she would not have been caught dead talking on a cell phone. She hated phones and resisted having one that could go with her everywhere, but finally, her move to Italy and the lack of a phone line in her antiquated apartment had convinced her it was time to join the twenty-first century.

But now she had to deal with her brother being able to reach her at any time of night and day.

"Hello, Trey."

"You have to tell Devan there will be no lavender in the wedding."

Ariel sighed. Her little brother would be the death of her. Her gay little brother, whom she'd mostly raised from the time she was six and he was three while their parents dropped acid or blissed out on some other drug trip, and who had nearly been the death of her countless times already.

"Is that how people are greeting each other these days?" she asked.

"Can we skip the small talk? I'm having a wedding emergency here."

She loved her brother, but trying to be his mother, father and big sister all rolled into one well-meaning package was exhausting at best, and a recipe for mental illness at worst.

"Is the color your partner's friends are wearing all that important? Do we really need to spend an hour talking about this?"

"The drag queens want to wear lavender bridesmaid dresses. It's a nightmare, Ariel. A nightmare."

Of course it was.

"Trey, I think you need to get a sense of proportion here. What matters is that you love each other and want to stand up in front of the people you care about to say your vows, right?"

"What*ever*." She could picture him perfectly. He was rolling his eyes at her.

"How about otherwise—are you two doing okay?"

"Sure, if you consider fighting constantly, not having slept together for three weeks, and, and—"

Ariel couldn't understand what Trey said next, because he burst into tears.

"It's going to be okay, you know. People get married all the time," she said, trying to sound soothing. "Your problem is you're both trying to be the bride."

He laughed through his sobs. "What's that supposed to mean?"

"In a hetero wedding, the guy usually backs off

and lets the woman do all the planning and choosing and stuff. He doesn't give a damn what color the bridesmaid dresses are."

"Why not?"

"Because he's a guy."

"Oh." Trey was sniffling now, and a bit calmer.

No one ever had or ever would mistake him for straight. Ariel had spent her entire childhood protecting him from the cruel outside world. Even in liberal, gay-friendly Northern California where they'd grown up, things had never been easy for a sensitive little boy who loved to play dress-up in pink gowns and carried a Barbie doll around instead of a football.

"Isn't there any room for compromise?"

"I just can't believe how stressful it is planning a wedding. I feel like we're in the midst of Middle East peace talks."

"That's a big clue you're taking it all too seriously. You should be having fun. It's supposed to be a happy day to celebrate that you love each other, not—"

"Not cause for divorce before we even tie the knot?"

She could hear the wry smile in his voice now. "Exactly."

As her brother said something about whether they were going to go strictly vegan or ovo-lacto-vegetarian for the wedding meal, Ariel glanced at her watch. She still had two hours before her latest job interview across town, and her stomach was already getting a little queasy at the idea of it not going well.

She'd worked all over Europe as an English tutor, but now that she was in Italy, she had to face the fact that her Italian was very limited, and all her interviewers so far had wanted someone with better Italian language skills. She tried to emphasize that her linguistic skills overall were superb and that she always picked up a solid grasp of a language within a month or two of being in a country.

But her pool of potential jobs was dwindling about as fast as her cash reserves, and she was beginning to feel a wee bit discouraged by it all.

Ariel said her goodbyes to her brother and closed her cell phone, then dropped it in her purse and stared at the embassy building where she was now standing. Somewhere along the way, she'd lost track of the guy she was stalking—no, make that following—and it occurred to her now that she didn't even care.

She plopped down on the fountain where she'd made a habit of sitting and watching people go by. Around her, pigeons loitered and fought over crumbs.

Another day had passed without her approaching the Italian guy, and she was getting more and more freaked out by her own lack of confidence. She needed to write, was what she needed. She needed to stop obsessing about men and write about the problem instead.

There was a shady café two blocks over where she had sat for a while the day before, and she was about to stand up and head toward it when she caught some movement next to her out of the corner of her eye. Ariel looked over to see a man staring at her and smiling.

He was gorgeous. Really, truly, stunningly gorgeous. Take-her-breath-away gorgeous.

"Good morning. You are American?" he said.

"Oh, God, how can you tell?" Ariel glanced down at herself.

She went to great pains not to look like a stereotypical American. She never wore jeans unless they were accompanied by high heels, never wore white sneakers and always, always stayed up with the latest European looks. Aside from the fact that it was fun to do, it ensured she didn't have to worry much about getting hassled by gypsies and pickpockets.

Besides, it was embarrassing as hell to be labeled an American in Europe before she'd even opened her mouth.

"Your face," he said. "It is, I would guess, an American face."

And his face—it was a work of art. Ariel didn't consider herself a woman easily swayed by typical beauty, but then, this guy was no typical beauty. His physical attractiveness was hard to pinpoint, but had everything to do with the spark of passion in his dark brown eyes. His hair, almost black, was wavy and long, brushing the collar of his shirt and tumbling over his forehead. The unruliness of it made a nice contrast to his starched white shirt and summer wool khakis. He had the slightest beard and the straightest, sexiest teeth she'd ever seen.

He looked to be somewhere between thirty-five and forty.

"What does that mean?" she finally managed to ask. But she couldn't stop staring at him now.

"You Americans, you are…how do you say… Mutts. Your features get all blended together and come out even and pretty, like cover models."

"So we're a nation of cover models?"

"Yes," he said, smiling as if he'd made some great revelation.

"Funny how most of the popular models today are not American though, huh?"

"That is because everyone wants the exotic new look, and you Americans have trouble looking exotic."

Another thing she loved about Rome—it was a place even the guys could talk fashion and beauty.

But there was something about this guy's voice… just a hint of an accent she couldn't place. Not wholly Italian.

"Are you Roman?" she asked.

"Not quite," he said. "My father worked in foreign service, and we traveled all over the world throughout my childhood."

"Ah. That explains your odd accent."

"And you? What brings you to this lovely fountain today?"

"Just wandering the city. I have a job interview later."

"For?"

"Teaching English to the children of a wealthy family."

"Is that what brought you to Rome?"

"Sort of. I've been moving around Europe for the past five years, just going wherever I want and teaching English to get by. I'm actually a writer, although not earning a living at it yet."

"And do you write epic love stories?" he said with a wry smile.

Ariel never revealed her blogging identity—her brother was the only one she'd ever told. Not even her closest friends knew about Sex As a Second Language…though perhaps that creepy anonymous poster number five knew the real Eurogirl. So she simply shrugged and said, "Sure, you could call them love stories."

"I'm very fascinated by the creative process. Perhaps you could tell me all about yours over dinner tonight."

She blinked. No one had ever accused a Roman man of subtlety when it came to women. And this guy, he made her head swim. Maybe this was why fate had led her to the embassy—not because she was supposed to be with the guy she'd been following every day, but rather because she was supposed to bump into…this guy. But it seemed way too good to be true.

"What's your name?" she said.

"Marco Antonetti. And you?" He extended one

large, perfectly sculpted hand to her, and she did the same.

But instead of shaking, he dipped his head, brushing his lips ever so slightly across the skin of her hand.

"Ariel," she said. "Ariel Turner."

Normally such blatant cheesiness as hand-kissing would have made her roll her eyes, but this Marco guy managed to pull it off. Perhaps it was the touch of irony in his expression even as he did it—a touch of irony that was always there, she suspected. It said he knew he was being a cliché and he was going to be one anyway, because some clichés were fun.

And maybe because—she hoped, she hoped, she hoped—he knew women really wanted all that grand romance stuff.

"I'd love to go to dinner," she heard herself saying and was surprised to hear herself sounding happy, enthusiastic, even.

"We will celebrate your getting a new job."

"Let's hope," she said.

"I have a feeling about this—they will take one look at you and know they must hire you."

"Wish I had your confidence."

"Do you live nearby?"

"Not far from the Spanish Steps," Ariel said, careful to be vague.

"Nice location."

"I will always choose to live in a hovel in the heart of the city rather than a nice place farther out."

And she had. Her apartment was one small room at the top of a rickety case of stairs that felt as if they were going to collapse at any moment. She shared a grungy bathroom with two other tenants, and the sounds of the city reverberated through the ancient walls day and night.

Still, she loved it. Loved that she could hear and feel the heartbeat of Rome all around her. She wanted to be immersed in the city, to smell it and breathe it and eat it and feel it.

"I know a place not far from there. How about we meet at the Spanish Steps at eight? We can go for drinks, then dinner?"

Drinks, then dinner, was code for "I want to loosen you up with alcohol to make sure we get down and dirty after dinner."

Lucky for Marco, a dry martini was Ariel's favorite way to start a first date. And a wet, wild, sweaty roll between the sheets was her favorite way to end it—with the right guy.

She hoped and prayed he was it—the guy who'd end her unlucky streak and give her a great wrap-up to her sexual memoirs. Even if he wasn't the one, perhaps he could be a nice warm-up lover to get her confidence back after her string of disasters.

"It's a date," she said, and for the first time all week, she felt hopeful.

3

When In Rome, Find a Roman to Do

I met a guy today. A hot, seemingly intelligent, available guy. Could he be the Italian dream lover I've been looking for?

Let's don't get our hopes up, people. I'm feeling a bit hesitant after the last guy. After all, who knows what atrocities might lurk within this Italian's pants?

Shall we take bets about what will go wrong next?

Comments:
1. Anonymous says: Wow, Eurogirl, you're sounding all jaded and stuff.

2. Eurogirl says: Sorry. I am, aren't I?

3. dogman says: Maybe he'll be hairless.

4. xta-c says: I've never seen a hairless guy. Do guys ever shave it all off down there?

5. TinaLee says: I dated a guy once who went through chemo and lost all his pubic hair.

6. Asiana says: Hairless is way sexy.

7. Eurogirl says: Asiana, you're kind of a weirdo, aren't you?

8. Asiana says: Yup.

9. dogman says: Asiana, if you're hot, I'll shave it all off for you.

MARC GAZED UP at the window that must have been Ariel's. She hadn't been hard to find. Once he knew the area, he had simply called the apartment buildings in the vicinity and talked to landlords until he found the one who'd rented to a new American tenant in the past week.

From there, it was easy to pry out an apartment number and address by making an excuse about being a friend. Italians weren't as paranoid about privacy or fearful of lawsuits as Americans were.

As he stood in the alleyway below her window, his dick went hard again thinking about her. A lamp shone through the window, and after a few minutes, he saw her pass by wearing a white bra and panties. His dick grew harder.

He had never slept with a woman for the sake of his mission. Doing so was not outside the realm of propriety, but it did trample a bit on his own personal code of ethics. He had been with enough women to know that newness and the excitement of the unknown were not nearly as thrilling as being with someone with whom he shared real intimacy.

But something about Ariel Turner thrilled him— made him want to toss aside personal ethics to discover all her deepest, darkest secrets. It wasn't just that she was pretty. Pretty women were a dime a dozen. It was some indescribable quality that came from the way Ariel carried herself and the spark in her eyes and the mysterious set of her mouth. She looked as if whatever secrets she had to reveal were utterly fascinating ones.

He wasn't sure what he'd hoped to learn by showing up at Ariel's place early and casing it. Just old habit. Living his entire adult life as a clandestine operative had made him paranoid in the extreme. He was distrustful of everyone, intensely private and always planning his next move.

In his world, everyone had a secret motive, a hidden truth and possibly some information he might need.

It didn't exactly make him a conventional guy, but there was no such thing as conventional in Marc's chosen career. He occasionally wondered if he'd ever give up the spy world for something more settled, but those thoughts faded away with the next big thrill.

So he'd turned into the kind of guy women left "bastard" messages for, the kind of guy who was planning to sleep with someone for the sake of his work. It wasn't how he'd ever envisioned himself, but then, when was life ever even remotely like anyone planned?

As he stared up at her window, he mentally shoved his conscience aside. There were worse tasks in the world than seducing a beautiful woman for the sake of national security, right?

Absolutely.

ARIEL HATED FIRST DATES. She pretty much tried her best to avoid them, but sometimes, a date was the only way to get from casual first-meet chitchat to down and dirty sex on the kitchen floor—or any variation thereof.

She paced across the room, flung open the closet door and stared at her sorry selection of clothes. The thing about being a vagabond of sorts was that she traveled lightly, and that meant she didn't possess the typical overflowing mess of a wardrobe. Rather, she had only the basics. But now that she was in one of the fashion capitals of the world, she definitely needed to go shopping.

It would have been nice to have thought of that before her date with Marco.

Okay, so… She had the standard little black dress and the standard little red dress. Red or black. Big decision. She went with black. Don't want to look like you're trying too hard.

That was the thing she hated most about dates. The artificiality of it all, the worries about appearances and trying or not trying and what to say and how to act and whether or not to show her hand or play it straight—or just go home and bury her head under the covers.

By the time she had her dress on, there was a thin film of perspiration covering her skin, so Ariel went to the window and leaned out in an effort to cool herself. She needed to buy a fan. There was no air-conditioning in the building, and if it was this hot in May, she was going to be seriously screwed come July.

Down below, the city bustled. Her view of the Spanish Steps was priceless. Teenagers gathered, flirted and generally clogged up foot traffic, while tourists stood around gawking and taking photos. She inhaled the muggy air and closed her eyes, letting the very faint breeze cool her a bit. But after a moment, she got the odd feeling she was being watched.

Ariel opened her eyes and scanned the scene below more carefully. The strange blog comment echoed in her head. Who could have known her true identity? Was it just some ill-timed joke, or did someone really know who she was and why she'd left Greece?

She thought of the way Marco had plopped down next to her on the fountain. Coincidence, or was he some hired hit man sent by Kostas to take her out? Ariel wondered—not for the first time—if the Greek police had taken her anonymous tip seriously.

She was starting to think like a true lunatic. This was Rome, after all. Men flirted as naturally as they breathed, and it wasn't exactly unheard of for them to ask women on dates. Marco was clearly Italian, so what could he possibly have to do with her Greek terrorist lover? Absolutely nothing.

But then some movement at the edge of her gaze drew her attention, and she looked over to see a man disappearing behind a building. A man who looked, if she wasn't mistaken, very much like Marco.

But he could not have known where she lived… could he? Perhaps he'd arrived early for their date. Yeah, that had to be it, if it had even been him she'd seen. More likely, it was one of the million other dark-haired men in the city.

Okay, so she wasn't going completely insane. Only partly.

She watched the spot where the man had vanished, but he never reappeared, and a glance at the clock on her nightstand told her she was going to be late if she didn't hurry up and finish dressing.

Fifteen minutes later, she was ready, and her cell phone rang just as she was slipping into high-heeled black sandals. She didn't recognize the number that popped up on the LCD, but she answered.

"Hey," a male voice said. "I'm early."

"Marco?"

"Yeah. I apologize for bugging you, but I was wondering if you'd prefer formal or casual for dinner. Sorry I forgot to ask earlier, but I could call and try to get a reservation now—"

"Casual is good. No need for a reservation."

"Are you okay? You sound a little tense."

"Sorry," Ariel said, blinking at the fact that he managed to read her voice. She didn't like sounding so transparent. "It's nothing."

Just the fear of death at the hands of a terrorist. Nothing much at all.

"I'm down here at the Steps whenever you're ready."

Ariel bit her lip and debated whether to be cautious or bold. It had never been a matter of debate in her head before. Bold had always been her middle name. But now…now suddenly she could barely recognize herself.

"Want to come up for a drink first?" she blurted in an effort to revive the former fun-loving Ariel.

Her stomach churned.

"Are you sure it's okay?"

"Absolutely," she said with enthusiasm she didn't feel at all.

"Okay, sure. What's your address?"

Against any shred of good sense she had, she gave it to him. This was her big chance to prove to herself she hadn't lost it, after all. Surely, the police had arrested Kostas already. And she could find out if Marco was really a decent lover before she had to suffer through an entire dinner with him. It was the kind of thing she wouldn't have hesitated to do a few months ago.

But now…

Before she could delve into her neuroses further,

he was standing at her apartment door, looking a little sweaty from the heat and the climb up four flights of stairs.

"What would you like to drink?" Ariel said as she stepped aside for him to come in. "I've got a fresh bottle of champagne in the refrigerator."

"That sounds great," he said, smiling. He leaned in and kissed her on each cheek, and she did the same.

But when they parted, she couldn't make herself move. She couldn't believe she had this guy in her apartment, and she wasn't sure if it was excitement or terror that immobilized her—or both.

Marco's gaze darkened as it roamed from her eyes downward, over her chest, her torso, her legs. He stopped at her feet and stared. "Nice shoes."

"I'll leave them on," she said as she reached behind her back and started to unzip her dress.

This was the kind of thing good old Ariel would do. Wasn't it? Sure it was. She'd always prided herself on her sexual boldness, her ability to decide what—and who—she wanted and go after it with a vengeance.

But her stomach rebelled against the idea. Something held her back. She kept thinking of Kostas, of how wrong she'd been about him, of fleeing Greece, of the blog comment.

Stress. She didn't deal well with it. She had spent her entire childhood under its crushing weight, and as soon as she'd gotten a chance to be free of it at the age of eighteen, she'd run—as fast and as far as she could.

She was still running.

"Kiss me," she whispered, hoping she sounded more forceful than she felt.

Marco closed the distance between them and slipped his hands around her waist. He pulled her against him, and she felt his erection. He kissed her. Long, slow, teasing at first and then deeper. Then deeper still, his tongue caressing hers, coaxing her and warming her and promising her more.

She moaned into his mouth as her body responded, blood rushing to sensitive places. And he pulled her closer still.

For a moment, she almost forgot the stress. That was what sex usually did for her. It made her forget everything but the moment, everything but the good feelings. It made her relax.

Marco smelled incredibly clean and male, with a hint of something like sage in his cologne. And he felt hard, unyielding—divine. She ran her hand along his jaw, letting his heavy five o'clock shadow tickle her fingertips, and imagined the feel of it against her naked flesh.

But something inside her still wanted to hold back.

"Is something wrong?" he asked, pulling away, his warm brown eyes searching hers.

An emotionally perceptive heterosexual male? Did such a creature really exist?

"No," she lied.

He looked as though he didn't believe her. "We don't have to rush this, you know. I'd rather we take it slow enough to at least enjoy the scenery."

"It's not that," she said. "I mean, I guess I'm just… I don't know. My last relationship was a bit of a disaster, and maybe it's got me feeling a little off-balance starting up with someone new."

"Then we definitely shouldn't rush things."

She forced a smile and slid her hands down his chest and beneath his pants to his cock. "But that's what I *do.* I don't know how to go slowly."

"Not that I'm complaining," Marco said. "But if we're going to end up in bed, we'll probably enjoy it a hell of a lot more if we know each other a bit first."

Ariel blinked. What kind of weird freaking role-reversal was this, anyway? Was she actually being talked out of easy sex by a *guy?* An Italian guy, no less?

"You really believe that?" she taunted as she gripped him and massaged.

"You don't?" he asked, looking both aroused at her touch and incredulous at her words.

She'd never even tried to take it slow. She'd lived her entire romantic life in fast-forward, but perhaps that wasn't exactly cool to admit on the first date.

So instead, she shrugged, and said, "I've been pretty satisfied with my method."

"I can see why." His voice grew ragged as she continued to toy with him. "But…"

"But you want to convince me there's something more? Deeper intimacy and all that?"

He breathed out, his gaze darkening again. Then he reached down and stilled her hand. "Yeah," he said. "I do."

And Ariel, for the first time in her adult life, wondered if she was missing out on something. Like any good adventurer, she made a mental vow to find out.

4

Status Report: So Far, *Sooooo* Good

It's probably bad form to stop in the middle of making out to post on my blog, but since when have I ever practiced good dating form?

Under the guise of checking my e-mail, I just want to let you, my loyal readers, know that the new guy, X, has been kissed, and he is an extremely good kisser.

Like, the kind of kisser who makes me want to peel my panties off.

Stay tuned…

Comments:
1. Asiana says: Tease! We need details.

2. Carissa Ann says: If he was a really good kisser, your panties would already be off, and he'd be kissing the parts that count.

3. B cool says: Carissa Ann, you're a 'ho.

4. calidude says: I'm glad somebody's getting some action tonight. It sure as hell ain't me.

5. lolo says: Ooh, I love when you give the blow-by-blow report, Eurogirl. I want a midsex report ASAP.

6. darwinwuzright says: What kind of guy lets you stop in the middle of kissing him to go check your e-mail? And what kind of girl would do that, anyway?

7. Carissa Ann says: I've been known to talk on my mobile and send text messages during sex. Don't take it personally. It's just sex in the information age.

8. NOLAgirl says: Texting during sex? I have to try that. Did the guy even notice?

9. Carissa Ann says: No.

10. NOLAgirl says: Typical. Probably too busy admiring his own weewee.

"HEY, WHAT ABOUT THAT champagne you mentioned? Want me to get it?" Marc said as he reentered Ariel's room.

He'd excused himself to go to the bathroom, taking the opportunity to cool down from their smoking-hot kiss, and now Ariel was sitting at her desk using a laptop computer, seeming utterly un-affected by his putting the brakes on their encounter.

When she heard his voice, she closed the computer and turned to him. "Sorry, just checking my e-mail," she said. "I'll grab the champagne."

He spotted a tiny efficiency refrigerator in the far corner of the room, next to a sink and a small countertop, which must have functioned as her kitchen.

"Guess you eat out a lot, huh?"

She smiled. "Yeah. This place is my excuse not to cook."

Marc watched as she opened up the fridge and peered inside it. "Oh, crap. This thing isn't even cold. The outlet must have shorted out again."

"Why don't we get out of here instead," he said, grateful for the chance to get out in public sooner, where they would be forced to practice a little restraint.

Not that he didn't want to fall right into bed with Ariel and do her like there was no tomorrow—he did, very much—but he also wanted to build a little trust between them. If she rushed into sex with him and then viewed him as a one-night stand because she was too embarrassed to face him the next day, his plan to get close to her would be ruined.

He'd seduce her first with trust, and then with his body.

"I'm sorry about the champagne—I had no idea this damn thing wasn't working."

"You hungry now? We can go straight to dinner if you want."

Ariel shrugged. "Why don't we go for a walk first, maybe find a drink along the way?"

"Okay." Marc smiled, glad she hadn't taken his pulling back the wrong way. Some women would have been affronted that he hadn't wanted to hop right into bed as soon as they'd said hello, and it had been a risky gamble for him to assume she wasn't one of those women.

She grabbed her purse and they headed out of her room and down the rickety staircase. A few minutes later, they were standing at the top of the Spanish Steps, among the throng of teenagers and tourists and everyday Romans out escaping the heat of their homes. Ariel looked entranced by it all.

"So you just moved to Rome—when did you get here?"

"About a week ago. I'm still in awe of everything."

"Is this your first time here?"

"No, I visited once on a whirlwind summer tour in college. I had a hangover for most of the waking hours of that trip, though, and remember very little, except that Rome entranced me like no other city ever has."

Marc smiled as he watched her face light up. He felt the same about the ancient city. It was an overwhelming rush of old and new, overflowing with people and noise and sights and smells.

The high-pitched whine of motor scooters racing through the streets contrasted sharply with the silent stateliness of the old Roman monuments. Everywhere one looked, there was some reminder that Rome had stood the test of time and was still thriving today.

"Have you seen any of the usual sights since you got here?"

"Only what I've passed by on my way to job interviews. I've been in a weird sort of funk lately."

Marc took her hand and led her down the steps. "Want to go for a walk to the Forum? It looks beautiful at sunset."

"Sure, a walk anywhere sounds good right now. I'd love to get a little tour from a local's perspective."

"I don't think anyone gets to call themselves a local until their family has lived in the city for six generations."

"Oh, right. Well, you're more of a local than I am."

Marc watched as a group of men they passed stopped in their tracks and turned to stare at Ariel. He glared back as a warning for them to keep their mouths shut, and they did.

"You must be getting a lot of male attention around here."

She cast a glance in the direction of the men. "Sure, I guess. Every female does."

"It doesn't hurt that you're stunningly pretty and wearing a sexy outfit."

Ariel smiled at him. "Thanks, and you can keep up the flattery for as long as you want, because I, for one, don't get tired of it."

"So how did your interview go today?"

"I'm not sure, but they didn't seem as uninterested as previous families. One of their sons is a teenager, and I kind of got the sense that they were hoping a female tutor would motivate him to actually study and improve his grades."

"Lucky kid. I wish I'd had a tutor like you back then. I might have been an A student."

Ariel laughed. "I don't do any extracurricular services. But I would like to work for this family. It's a direct twenty-minute bus ride from my apartment, and their house is amazing."

"Air-conditioned?"

"It was so big and had so much marble in it, I'm not even sure. Let's just say it was worlds apart from my little hovel."

"Hey, maybe they'd offer you a room if the job goes well. That's not unheard of around here."

She shook her head. "No way. I tried the live-in-tutor-slash-nanny gig once and won't do it again."

"Too close for comfort?"

"Way too close. I was miserable having such intimate knowledge of other people's lives, for one thing, and for another, the father hit on me. That was the end of that job."

"Where was this?"

"In Barcelona. My first tutoring job. After that, I've stayed strictly a visiting tutor. Sometimes I work for multiple families, and sometimes, like if I get this gig, I'm lucky to have a wealthy family and just work for them."

They were walking south along the main drag, toward the famous sites. To their left, traffic was backed up on the street for as far as the eye could see.

"So what is it that you write? You never answered me earlier."

A mysterious smile crossed her lips, then vanished, and Marc wondered if she'd tell him the truth. He'd taken a quick glance at her blog earlier, before their date, and a scan of the archives had proven to be very intriguing indeed. Ariel was either good at making up stories, or she was quite the sexual adventurer.

He wasn't sure which he was hoping would be true.

"I write memoirs. Sort of travel memoirs, I guess you would say."

"Like about the scenery and stuff?" he managed to say with a straight face. After all, maybe she really did write travel memoirs in addition to her sex blog.

"Yeah, the scenery and culture and all that."

"So that's why you've been traveling around Europe all these years?"

"Not exactly. The travel is just for the sake of it. I wanted to get away from the U.S. for a while, and I wanted to really get to know Europe. The writing is more of a by-product."

"I'd love to read your work sometime."

From what he'd read thus far, she was quite the talented writer—she had an astonishing talent for making his dick hard with the written word. He wondered if she ever let her lovers in on the fact that she was blogging about them.

And then it struck him like a blow to the head. If he became her lover, she'd likely be blogging about him next. Did he really want to know what she'd say about him when she didn't think he was reading?

He'd always considered himself a good lover, but he'd never been privy to an unbiased review on his sexual performance. Could his fragile male ego take it if the reviews weren't all raves?

Maybe Ariel was just the sort of wake-up call a serial dater like himself needed. Maybe he'd think twice about going through women like flavors of the month if he saw his exploits emblazoned on the Internet for all the world to read.

She was saying something, and he realized he'd spaced out. "—Don't normally let people read my rough drafts."

"Do you have anything published yet?"

She cast him an odd look, and he wondered if she'd addressed the issue while he'd been thinking. "A few things, in magazines and on the Internet."

From inside her purse came a tinny version of the song "Jungle Boogie."

"Sorry," she said. "That's my phone. I should get it."

She dug out a small silver phone and answered it in Italian tinged with an American accent. He listened as she spoke to what must have been a member of the family she'd interviewed with earlier that day. When she paused to listen, she shot him a thumbs-up sign and smiled.

A minute later, she was thanking the person on the phone and saying goodbye. She closed up the mobile phone and dropped it in her bag again.

"I got the job, starting Monday! They want me to tutor at least through the summer while the kids are out of school, which works out well for my plans, since I'll be returning to the U.S. in the fall."

"Congratulations. We'll have to have a celebratory drink to toast your new job."

Ariel smiled. "I didn't realize how stressed out I was getting about my lack of a regular paycheck, but suddenly I really do feel like celebrating."

"I told you you'd get the job."

"I've been feeling a little depressed lately, so I really needed the good news."

"Depressed about not finding a job right away?"

"About everything. Midlife crisis, I guess."

They reached the path that led to the Roman ruins, just in time for the waning light to cast the scene in gold. Tourists were sparse at this time of day—as were the pickpockets, making it the perfect time to visit. Marc didn't hit the tourist sights much—only when someone from out of town came to visit, which was rare for a covert CIA operative.

"You don't exactly look like you've reached midlife. How old are you? Twenty-five?"

She laughed. "Good answer. I'm thirty, actually. Maybe it's a one-third life crisis."

"Hey, I'm forty, and I'm kind of going through the same thing, to be honest."

"Wow, so I'm on a date with an old guy, huh?"

"Haven't you ever heard about the fragility of the male ego?"

"I'm kidding!"

They reached a bend in the path and the entire ruins of the Forum were visible. She stopped in her tracks.

"Wow. Gorgeous."

"Told you this was a good time to visit."

"Didn't the sign say this closes at sundown?"

"Yeah, that's the downside. We can't stick around for long, but it's worth the walk to see the light like this, don't you think?"

Ariel gazed out at the scene of towering pillars and crumbling stone walls. "Definitely."

He took the opportunity to slide his hand around her waist and pull her close. When he dipped his head and kissed a spot right above her eye, she pulled back a bit and cast him a coy look.

"I thought you were going to teach me all about deeper intimacy and stuff."

"I doubt there's anything I could teach you that you don't already know."

"So you were just playing the tease? Is that something you old guys learn to do?"

"I resent being labeled an old guy," he said. "I'm not exactly popping Viagra, you know."

"I wouldn't know. You didn't let me find out, remember?"

"I really did just want to talk to you and get to know you a bit. Is that so bad?"

"I know, I know. You want to show me that you're a thoroughly evolved male, only interested in sex as part of a complete relationship package."

Marc opened his mouth to protest, but she'd managed to stun him into silence. She'd nailed him. She'd seen right through his MO.

Maybe he really had met his match.

"Isn't that what women want?" he finally said.

"You can't make a blanket statement about what women want any more than I can make a blanket statement about how you old guys operate." Her mischievous smile said she was just goading him now.

Rather than have her nail him about his dating modus operandi any further, he decided to change the subject.

"What's the biggest age difference you've had in a relationship?"

"Depends on how you define relationship. I tend to keep mine mostly about sex, to be honest."

"Okay, so let's be blunt—what's the oldest guy you've slept with?"

"I was twenty-one and he was forty-eight."

"Wow. You really do know about us old guys."

She laughed. "That was a fluke. I don't discriminate by age, though. I just go with whomever interests me—dated a nineteen-year-old for a few months when I was twenty-nine."

"You're pretty open-minded."

"I've never been able to equate how well I get along with someone with how old they are. It has much more to do with individual lifestyles and states of mind than it does any number we put on ourselves."

"Just so you know, I'm not put off by your shockingly underage self."

"Thank you for being so open-minded. I promise I don't wet the bed or suck my thumb."

"Hey, neither do I."

Then Ariel stood on her tiptoes, placed her hands on his chest and kissed him. Her tongue danced along the edges of his lips, then slipped into his mouth. He opened up to her and tasted her, savored her wet warmth, slid his hands around her and pulled her close, where she could feel his growing erection.

Marc watched her as they kissed; her eyes were closed as she pressed against him. He watched, as some inner voice in his head told him he was getting into something he couldn't control. His career had taught him to always look for controllable variables, always assert one's will where it could be asserted.

But Ariel knew how to play the game, too, he suspected. And what if she was a better player than he was? What if she was always thinking one step ahead of him, or could see his next move before he made it? He'd never been with a woman he didn't think he could play before, and as much as the prospect threw him off balance, it also thrilled him as he'd never been thrilled before.

5

Status Report: So Far, *Soooo* Good

Comments continued…
11. calidude says: Way too much male bashing happening on this blog. I'm gonna take my wee-wee and go play somewhere else if you girlies don't chill.

12. Asiana says: Sorry, calidude. You're right. Some guys don't deserve to be bashed. Well, a few of them…I mean, there must be one somewhere.

13. calidude says: See what I mean? I'm outta here.

14. mr crispy says: If we weren't all such assholes, women wouldn't talk trash about us.

15. Carissa Ann says: Amen, mr crispy.

16. tanenbaum says: Since Eurogirl's not here to defend the spirit of the blog (I'm trying not to be disgruntled that she's probably off getting laid

while I'm sitting here preparing to whack off to some Internet porn), I just want to point out that she mostly writes stuff about loving men, not dissing them.

17. calidude says: tanenbaum, you just want to have cybersex with Eurogirl.

ARIEL SAT DOWN on a boulder and inhaled the thick evening air. Kissing Marco was making her dizzy, or maybe she was just dehydrated. She'd been amused at his efforts to put on the brakes earlier, when he'd first arrived at her apartment, but she hadn't been fooled.

He was one of those guys who thought they had a more refined sense of how to play the dating game, that was all. He thought she'd be more intrigued by him if they went through the motions of getting to know each other, acting interested in each other's lives and blah blah blah.

And that was fine with her. She liked hearing people's stories, although she was pretty far past thinking the whole getting-to-know-you dance was anything but a well-rehearsed act people put on to try to impress each other. The real getting to know each other happened so subtly and so slowly that most people never stuck around to let it happen, including her.

Marco sat down beside her, and when she looked over at the foot traffic passing by on the nearest sidewalk, she could have sworn she spotted Kostas. Her stomach twisted, and she leaped up from the rock to get a better look. But all she could see was a group of Japanese tourists exiting a bus parked at the curb. No tall, attractive Greek men in sight.

Weird. It must have been that strange post on her blog that had her seeing ghost ex-boyfriends now in her paranoia.

From down below, she heard a tiny yowl. She and Marco looked toward the sound, and a silver kitten emerged from a dark space in the ruins and blinked up at them.

"Rome is famous for its stray cats," Marco said, and Ariel nodded, hoping he was assuming that the kitten was why she had acted like a deranged jack-in-the-box.

"I've seen the calendars and postcards around the tourist shops," she said, "along with the live strays living everywhere."

"I tried to adopt one once, but it ran away first chance it got," he said.

"I've never had a pet," Ariel admitted.

She was allergic to caring for things, she liked to say. But it was more that she'd used up all her maternal instincts on her brother, and she had nothing left to give.

"Not even a goldfish? Not even as a kid?"

She shook her head. "My parents weren't exactly fit to care for animals, let alone children."

He nodded sympathetically. "I'm sorry."

The kitten had taken to circling Ariel's ankle and butting its head up against her shin. Its pointy little face was almost too much to bear. She reached down and petted it gingerly, afraid of breaking it.

"*C'est la vie,* right?"

"Looks like she likes you," he said, smiling at the cat.

"I probably smell like food."

She let the cat nuzzle its face into her palm, and it began licking her with its raspy little tongue. She laughed at the weird sensation. "I don't think I've ever really even been around a cat before. I had no idea their tongues felt like concrete."

She looked up at Marco and found him staring at her, a mysterious smile playing on his lips.

"What?" She suddenly felt self-conscious.

"You're gorgeous," he said. "It's hard not to look at you."

"I could say the same about you." And she could. He was stunning, and not in the typical calendar guy way. His features weren't pretty, but he was beautiful nonetheless. Rough-hewn and all male.

"Thank you," he said, not managing to look the slightest bit modest.

"So tell me about your midlife crisis—maybe we can compare crisis notes."

The cat was attempting to climb up Ariel's leg now. It made more yowling sounds until she reached down and awkwardly scooped it up. Okay, so she wasn't going to get the animal lover of the year award anytime soon, but at least she could give the cat a little affection.

"It's nothing all that outlandish. I'm not feeling the urge to buy a Ferrari or grow a ponytail—"

"Your hair is already long," she pointed out, smiling. "And very sexy, by the way."

"Oh, right," he said, reaching back, pretending to be surprised he had hair.

"And you've never settled down, so you have no need for a Ferrari to make yourself feel all wild again."

"True. I guess it's a little odd to realize I'm probably halfway through my life. I start wondering if I should be doing anything differently, or doing something more than I am."

"I know what you mean," Ariel said, thinking of the weird malaise that had settled over her right before her thirtieth birthday last January and had never quite gone away. "I guess those round-number birthdays are natural times to reevaluate our lives and stuff."

"So what kind of crisis did you have?" he asked, watching as the cat rubbed its mangy little head against her belly and kneaded her lap with its paws.

It felt as though it was all fur and bones, and its light gray hair was matted in places. Ariel felt something in her belly like a maternal pang—a feeling she normally reserved for her brother.

"I sat around wondering if I was wasting my life away, mostly."

"Yeah, me, too."

"And my little brother announced his engagement around the same time, so it was weird, knowing he was moving on to this new phase of his life, while my life has virtually remained unchanged my entire adulthood."

"Except geographically, right?"

"Sure, I've traveled all over, but even that develops a sameness after a while, you know?"

He nodded. "Another new place, another foreign culture, another set of challenges."

"Somehow it all becomes the same stuff after a while."

"Do you ever want to settle down?"

"Settle down and what? Die?" She tried to keep her tone light to hide how much she bristled at the question she'd heard a million times.

"I should be the last person asking that question," Marco admitted. "I hear it too often myself."

"What do you say to it?"

"I say I like not knowing what the future holds too much to settle down."

"Good answer. Is it true?"

Marco shrugged, staring at the kitten who had settled in a ball in Ariel's lap now. "Sometimes it is. Sometimes it isn't."

"And lately it's more untrue, I bet."

"Because there's less future left, maybe. And maybe in my old age I'm starting to realize just having a big question mark in my future isn't the be-all and end-all."

"So then you have to find some other punctuation mark you can embrace as well as the question mark."

"Looks like you've got yourself a good little friend there," Marco said, ignoring her statement and nodding at the kitten.

"Just what I need."

"You could take it home, you know. Maybe you'd have better luck than I did."

"I don't even know if pets are allowed in my building."

"Are you kidding? This is Italy. Pets are allowed everywhere. You can probably take them into the hospital for surgery with you."

Ariel's lap was covered in cat hair now, and her skirt had little snags all over it from the kitten's claws. "It would just run away if I brought it home."

"It's young enough that it might not. You'd be saving it from a short life of scrounging for scraps from tourists and being the victim of bad cat post-card photography."

The kitten was approximately the size of Ariel's hand. Something so small and vulnerable didn't belong in her life. She sucked at taking care of things, her brother being the exception. Well, she'd mostly sucked at taking care of him, too, but he'd somehow survived her shoddy efforts.

"What would I do with a cat? I'll probably hardly ever be home to keep it company."

And yet, some part of her was enjoying the distraction from the other issues in her life, like the ex-boyfriend she'd just imagined walking by.

"You give it some food, you leave the window open for it to go out and do its business, you pet it once in a while. It's not hard."

She cast him a doubtful glare. "Why are you trying to talk me into keeping the cat, midlife crisis guy?"

"I'm living vicariously?"

"That's your midlife crisis? That you want a pet and are afraid to get one?"

"Not exactly."

"So what is it then?"

He shrugged and sat down next to her on the crumbling stone. "I'm too busy wallowing in general angst over the meaning of life to know what the outcome is."

"The meaning of life is to take care of the people around you. Or something like that."

"And the cats around you?"

"Probably," Ariel said with a sinking feeling.

Goddamn it. She didn't want anything to care for. She didn't want any responsibilities. She didn't want anything to tie her down.

And yet…she kind of did.

MARC GUIDED ARIEL through the fading throng of tourists and back toward her neighborhood. They needed to deposit the cat at her apartment, then buy some food for it and get it settled into its new home.

She carried the kitten in her arms as they walked, and Marc felt inordinately happy that she'd decided to keep the thing.

He was turning into a total sap in his pathetic middle age.

He stared down at the tiny kitten and felt a lump in his throat.

Total. Freaking. Sap.

He probably just needed to get laid. That was all.

If the meaning of life was to take care of the people around him, as Ariel had said, Marc found himself very much wanting to take care of her. What kind of trouble had she gotten into by consorting with a terrorist? Was she in danger? Was she a danger to anyone else? Did a person with such a simple and profound life mission have it in herself to support terrorism?

His gut said no. But he knew better than to trust anything, even his own gut, at this stage of the game. Better to proceed with caution than to charge forward and get his head lopped off by some danger lurking around the corner.

They stopped at a store, bought seven cans of cat food and continued on to Ariel's apartment building. Marc followed her up the stairs, his gaze fixed on her ass the entire way, and by the time they reached the top, he had a raging hard-on that was impossible to conceal in his pants. His only hope was that she wouldn't look down.

Fortunately, the cat had her attention. As soon as

she placed the sleeping animal on the couch, it sprang to life and darted across the room, freaked out by its new surroundings.

"Maybe just put some food out for it and leave it alone for a while to adjust, huh?" he said.

She took the cat food to the little cabinet and sink that made up her tiny kitchen, and a few seconds later the air was heavy with the scent of fish.

The kitten stuck its head out from under the couch and sniffed the air, then got spooked by some other unknown thing, maybe the leg of a table, and darted back into the darkness again.

Ariel placed the dish of food on the ground, along with a bowl of water, and then washed her hands. "What about cat litter?" she said. "We forgot that."

"Oh, right. I was thinking you'd be letting the cat go outside, but maybe not when it's this young, huh?"

She made a face. "Crap."

"We'll go buy some quick, no big deal."

They hurried back to the store and picked out a shallow plastic tub and a bag of litter, then came back to the apartment again. Ariel set up the litter box in a corner under the window, while Marc hunted down the kitten, tugging it out from behind a bookshelf to show it where it could do its business. The cat took one look at the litter it had been dropped into and darted back out and across the room.

"You think she'll know what to do with it?"

"Probably. Cats usually don't need any training.

They just head straight for the nearest gravelly surface that they can bury stuff in."

"So I guess that means my bed is safe. As long as she doesn't do her business on my pillow, we should get along fine."

Marc normally would have been feeling a little freaked out at such domesticity on the first date, especially a date that was supposed to be part of a mission, but somehow, all this cat homemaking felt pretty natural with Ariel. He watched her, and his body reacted in its own animal way. He wanted her more than he'd wanted any woman in a long time, and he felt comfortable with her in a way he hadn't felt in longer than he could remember.

Which was really screwed, given his reason for being with her. He needed to keep that in the forefront of his mind—terrorist ties, unclear motive for hanging out in front of the embassy…. She was probably nothing but trouble.

Which was normally what Marc thought of himself with regard to women. It was a weird change of pace having to think such a thing about the woman he was with.

He'd stepped into some alternate reality where the women were dangerous and he was a guy who wanted to bring home a kitten. Maybe he was trying to soften her up in his own mind, to make her into someone kinder than she really was….

But she'd gone along with it, so that said something about her character, didn't it?

Much as his work had taught him to trust no one, it had also taught him to trust his gut about people, and his gut told him Ariel was a more substantial person that she might be leading the world to believe.

But why? Why would she put up a shallow facade? To keep people from getting too close? He thought of what she'd said about her upbringing, and he wondered how much that had warped her ability to let people in.

Marc glanced at his watch and saw that it was nearly nine o'clock now. "You must be hungry by now. Want to go eat?"

Ariel washed her hands in the sink. "In spite of that cat food smell, I'm starving," she said.

Marc led her to a small trattoria he'd been to a few times, only a block from Ariel's apartment, where the food was simple but excellent.

When they were seated at a small table beside the front window, she said, "So tell me about your work."

And this was the part where he had to lie through his teeth. Normally, lying was such a habit he could do it without remorse, but suddenly, he found himself hesitating, not wanting to do what he knew he had to do to complete the mission.

"Not a lot to tell," he said. "I've worked at embassies all over the world." Which wasn't that far from the truth.

Ariel's eyes sparked with interest then. "What was your favorite location?"

"Maybe Rome, or believe it or not, Naples."

"Wow, Napoli's kind of rough, isn't it?"

"I just like how real and raw it is compared to the rest of the European cities I've been to."

"So you grew up mostly in Italy?"

"All over, really. I guess the travel bug got in my veins back then, and I couldn't imagine staying in one place for too long."

Watching Ariel across the table, her face lit by the candle that flickered between them, he was having a hard time forming complete sentences, let alone reciting his cover story for why he was living in Rome.

He wanted her so badly now, wanted to flick his tongue in that little valley between her tits, wanted to know how she tasted all hot and wet inside her panties, he felt like kicking himself for having put the brakes on earlier. What the hell had he been thinking?

Oh. Right. He was supposed to be gaining her trust. She was supposed to be a terrorist consort and all that. And he was supposed to be thinking with some other head besides the one between his legs.

Damn it.

The waiter came to take their order, and Marc breathed a silent sigh of relief. Hopefully he was done evading her questions for now, and maybe the menu would distract him enough to get his thoughts away from sex.

For now.

6

Status Report # 2: Houston, We Have Liftoff

I know, this is tacky. Utterly tacky. I am in the middle of a first date and risking all to report in to you, my dear, loyal readers. I hope you're feeling the love. And no, calidude, none of my actual readers ever have or ever will feel the love from me in the way you were implying—at least none that I'm aware of. Not even in cyberspace.

Anyway. X is in the bathroom, and I just have to say, holy crap he's got a hot body. And a veryveryvery nice package, I must say, judging by what I've felt beneath his clothes. Any minute now, I will be seeing it—er, I mean, him—naked.

Stay tuned for the next installment of Eurogirl's Date That We All Very Much Hope Won't Suck.

Comments:
1. Yoshi says: I'm loving the blow-by-blow (so to speak), Eurogirl. Can you report in again in the middle of your first orgasm?

2. Asiana says: I'm thinking that actual blogging in the middle of a first date, let alone in the middle of an orgasm, is a serious breach of dating etiquette. Let's don't expect too much from our hapless heroine.

3. milomar says: This sucks! I need more details.

4. gigi says: Eurogirl, good luck. I hope only the parts that are supposed to suck, suck.

"HEY, MORE E-MAIL?" Marco asked as he reentered the room.

Ariel shrugged and tried to look casual. "Sorry, I guess I'm addicted. It's my one little lifeline to the U.S."

He crossed the room as she closed the laptop. As she stood up, he pulled her to him.

"So," he whispered. "About where we left off earlier…"

"You mean with the gnocchi? Or the champagne toast?"

"I mean before dinner and before the cat—when I first got here," he said, tracing his fingers along her jawline, tickling her.

"Speaking of the cat, I found it lodged under the sofa cushion, so be careful where you sit."

"I will."

"Do we know each other well enough yet to take

it to the next level of intimacy?" she asked, her voice dripping sarcasm.

"Are you making fun of me?"

"I'm just wondering when you're going to drop the suave, gallant Italian guy act and admit you wanted to sleep with me as soon as you got here earlier."

"Of course I wanted to. Don't I get a little credit for using restraint?"

"No."

"You're a tough audience. I was just trying to be a little bit of a gentleman."

"You don't need to put on an act with me. I prefer that we both be up front about why we're here."

"Which is?"

"For sex."

He was trailing his fingers down her neck and over her breasts, making it hard to concentrate.

"Are you really just checking your e-mail on that computer, or are you reporting in to your superiors about me?" he asked with a wry smile, and Ariel's stomach flip-flopped.

If only he knew...

"My superiors? You mean the guys from my home planet?"

"It's just odd how you start typing on that thing every time I leave the room."

Ariel felt a film of perspiration form on her upper lip. She needed to stop with the status reports, clearly. She'd never gotten busted by a lover about her blog before, and she didn't intend to start now.

The whole idea of any guy she was sleeping with having such access to her sexual psyche gave her the heebie-jeebies. That was a level of intimacy she had no desire to achieve. She liked her guys at emotional arm's length.

Never mind that she let the whole world in on her sexual thoughts and experiences. That was under the guise of anonymity, and it was an outlet she enjoyed tremendously—the chance to be intimate without any of the messy side effects of intimacy. Having a guy she was actually having sex with happen along and get involved in the mix would be too much. She didn't want anyone that much inside her head, because she knew it would make her close up. It would kill her ability to write without emotional inhibition on the blog.

She tried to look apologetic. "I promise I'll stop being an e-mail addict, if you'll shut up and kiss me."

And he did.

Marco, of the long hair and the five o'clock shadow beard, of the security guard uniform and the strange accent, kissed her so well she went limp in his arms, and he eased her down onto the bed. Then he stretched out on top of her, and she wrapped her legs around him, holding him right where she wanted him.

"So you don't want me to be a gentleman?" he whispered.

"Hell, no."

"What do you want me to be?"

"A lover. It's very simple. You want me, right? You want to be inside me right now?"

"Yes," he said with a ragged sigh.

She could feel his hard dick pressing against her. It was no big secret what either of them wanted, but she felt as if she needed to rid him of a few antiquated notions about male-female relationships.

"And I want you inside me. We don't have to dance around that fact, do we?"

He rested on one elbow and regarded her with an inscrutable expression. "Is that all you want?"

"Right now, yes."

"And what if I want to know you? To really know you outside of bed, too?"

Ariel got that flip-floppy feeling in her stomach again. She shouldn't have been vulnerable to the idea of a not-so-casual relationship. She never really had been.

But right now, at this weird, unsteady moment in her life, he was hitting her where it hurt. And maybe he knew it, because he was in that unsteady moment, as well.

She sighed, but it sounded more like surrender than exasperation. "I guess I'd have to let you know me, then. Because you've got me right where you want me."

"Good," he said, then placed a soft kiss on her cheek. "Because I do want to know you."

Maybe she should have seen how good or bad he

was in bed before she agreed to a second date, but something about Marco stole away Ariel's will to resist.

He sat up and helped her out of her dress, then rid himself of his own clothes, while she sat back and admired him—all of him. He had a body just as gorgeous naked as it had been clothed. Just as she'd suspected.

Her gaze traveled over him, memorizing his planes and angles, his dips and curves and especially his hard parts. His erection jutted out toward her, and she couldn't help crawling across the bed to get better acquainted.

Sitting on the edge of the bed, she pulled him between her legs as he stood in front of her, and she took him into her mouth a little at a time, first his head, then his shaft, then all of him at once.

He buried his fingers in her hair and expelled a ragged breath. "Damn it," he muttered.

But before she could really savor him, he pulled away and pushed her down on the bed again, climbing on top of her.

"I wasn't finished," she whispered.

"Too bad," he said, his eyes glazed with desire. "You can do that later."

She watched as Marco put on a condom and positioned himself between her legs. She should have been doing something, she thought, but all she could do was lie in wait, paralyzed by her own desire.

And then she lost all sense of coherence when he pushed his dick inside her and began moving.

Ariel didn't believe in great sex the first time around. She tried to give most guys some leeway with regard to the early bedroom moves. If it came out great, it was usually a fluke.

Marco needed no leeway. He had all the right moves. He had moves she hadn't even encountered before.

And she'd encountered more than her share.

Ariel closed her eyes and gasped as he plunged deeper into her, his cock creating the sweetest kind of friction inside her.

She loved getting to know a new lover's body, but with Marco, it felt as if they already knew each other. As if they'd already done this dance before. They were in sync better than she could have hoped.

She opened her eyes again and watched him watching her as he moved inside her. His eyes were still glazed with desire and his hair hung forward, disheveled, partly hiding his face. She'd always loved a guy with long hair, but he took it to a whole other level. He made her fixate on his looks, his face, his beauty.

She hadn't been this attracted to a guy since… ever.

The thought scared the hell out of her and excited her at the same time.

She felt herself growing wetter as she came close to orgasm, and she wanted to hold off. It was way too soon. She wanted to savor the buildup some more.

She sat up and urged him back a bit, then turned around and offered herself to him.

He didn't waste any time sliding into her again, and she sighed at the delicious sensation of it. He held her hips tight as he pumped into her again, at first slowly, and then building up to a pace that had her moaning at the pleasure of it.

How could she ever get enough of him?

He was her wildest fantasy and her deepest desire, rolled into one package.

A dangerous combination for a girl who didn't want to get addicted.

She could feel his cock getting harder inside her, as he prepared to come, and she backed off, denying him his release for a while longer. She'd show him that restraint was most definitely worth practicing.

Ariel arched her hips and worked herself over him, slowly, slowly, forcing him to go at her pace. His gasps of pleasure suggested he didn't mind that she'd taken a bit of control. And for a while, he seemed content with that.

But when she could tell he was getting close again, he grasped her hips and forced her to hold still and then he leaned forward and slipped one hand between her legs, massaging her clit. She was wet, and his fingers glided over her in a delicious rhythm that started her body coiling tighter and tighter until she was about to come.

Then he pulled away.

"Two can play at that game," he whispered.

Still holding her tight, he showered her back with kisses, then flipped her over. "I want to see your face when you come," he said.

Ariel should have had some witty retort, but she could only lie there, weak with desire, aching for him to be inside her again. As if he could read her mind, Marco eased into her, covered her mouth with a kiss and continued making love to her at a torturously slow pace. He knew just the angle to enter her so that he was rubbing against her G-spot, and she could feel herself getting close to orgasm again.

So deliciously close. She moaned into his mouth, grasping his ass tight, holding on for dear life as she neared the edge.

And then she was there. Colors exploded behind her eyelids and her body was racked with pleasure, as she cried out, gasping as the waves of the orgasm rocked through her, over and over, going on longer than she could have imagined as he continued that deliciously slow movement inside her, as he watched her face, seeming to savor her pleasure as if it was his own.

When her orgasm passed, he quickened his pace, pumping hard into her, his own expression so calm it was as if he was deep in meditation, nearing a state of nirvana. Then his body tensed, and his orgasm coursed through them both, powerful and long, ending with him panting and limp on top of her, dripping sweat and kissing her hungrily.

"Wow," she whispered. "You're amazing."

"You are," he said, easing back to look her in the eye. "I think we're only just getting started. The best is yet to come, so to speak."

Maybe he was right. Maybe she'd finally found her perfect lover. Did she really dare to hope?

Of course, everything came with a catch, including Marco.

From across the room, the kitten yowled, then darted out and jumped onto the bed. When it caught sight of Ariel and Marco lying there together, it skidded to a halt and darted away in terror. They looked at each other and laughed, and Ariel was reminded all over again how surreal this night had been.

Somehow, in the space of a few hours, she'd gone from being an unemployed, unattached writer with depression issues, to being gainfully employed, potentially attached and the reluctant owner of a cat. Maybe still depressed, but also, now, bewildered by so many turns of events in one night. And underneath it all, a knot in her belly that wouldn't go away ever since she'd imagined spotting Kostas on the streets of Rome. What if he'd managed to hunt her down somehow?

No, she was going crazy. He couldn't have found her here. He was probably in jail.

At least the sex with Marco had been good. That

was the one turn of events she could point to as undoubtedly positive. Well, except that he had said he wanted to do the getting-to-know-each-other-better thing—and he seemed to really mean it.

7

First Date Sex

Under normal circumstances, there should be special allowances for the first time you have sex with someone. We fumble, we bump the wrong parts together, we clink teeth against teeth, we rub too hard or too softly, we come too fast or too slowly. We generally—and I mean "we" in the global sense—don't do such a great job.

And yet, every once in a while a first encounter comes along that blows all other first encounters out of the proverbial water.

Last night was just such an occasion.

Yes, loyal readers, you heard it here first. My bad-luck-in-bed streak seems to have passed. Thank God. I was beginning to get a complex.

Seriously. I was.

Somewhere around my third orgasm, I realized the tide had turned. The date definitely was not sucking, at least not in a bad way.

I don't mean to sound like a braggart. It was mostly his skill, anyway, that made things so great. Good sex, after all, is like dancing with a partner who knows all the same steps as you and whom you've been practicing with for weeks. So it comes as no surprise that it usually takes a while to get in the groove with a new partner.

So the new guy, X, can do things with his tongue that are probably outlawed in many parts of the world. Or at least they're so much fun that they should be.

And are you aware that if you achieve full suction on the clitoris, an orgasm can be produced in a matter of seconds?

I actually learned stuff last night. I mean, me. Learned. Something. New.

I didn't think that was possible anymore, but this, I promise you, was an occasion where I was thrilled to be proven wrong.

Comments:

1. ReneeDupree says: Full suction? You mean like airtight?

2. carrieann says: I just tried that—er, I mean, my boyfriend and I did—and it works! Thank you Eurogirl. You're my new best friend.

3. benet says: Wow. I did, too. Totally unfreaking believable.

4. Eurogirl says: Yikes, we're starting to sound like

a sex toy infomercial here. But truly, the testimonials are fun to hear. I'm glad to spread my little gems of wisdom, on the rare occasions when I have any.

5. timberwolf says: I need to find a girlfriend so I can try it. Any takers?

6. lola says: send me your pic, timberwolf. :-)

7. Eurogirl says: timberwolf, the next girl you try it on will suddenly love you like there's no tomorrow.

8. B cool says: I wonder if that trick works on the dick, too.

9. Eurogirl says: I don't think so. I tried it.

10. B cool says: Oh, well. So dicks are harder that way. Pardon the pun.

11. cayenne says: Congrats on the end of your bad luck streak, Eurogirl.

12. MenaB says: Yeah, we should have a blog party or something to celebrate.

13. Anonymous says: Eurogirl, I hope you're practicing safe sex. I know how reckless you can be, and I wouldn't want you putting yourself in even more danger than you're already in.

14. MenaB says: Jeez, Anonymous, why don't you ride your high horse somewhere else?

15. Eurogirl says: Although condoms can't protect me from the danger of having bad sex, I do always, always insist my lovers wear them for the obvious reasons we all know about, because we're all smart, responsible adults, right?

MARC WOKE UP TO the warm glow of the morning sun and the sound of footsteps outside the window, which was impossible…because weren't they on the fourth floor?

He peered with one eye out the window and saw a dark, swarthy man wearing a hard hat and a tool belt staring back at him. Alarmed, he sat up in bed and started to get out to investigate further, until he realized he was buck naked.

Okay, Plan B. He yelled at the man in Italian to get the hell away from the window, and the man obeyed reluctantly, his gaze lingering on Ariel's bare shoulder a moment too long for Marc's taste.

"Bastard," he muttered under his breath as Ariel stirred and opened her eyes.

"What's wrong?" she said.

"Is somebody working on this building? There was just a construction guy outside your window."

She frowned in confusion. "No. Well, I mean, I don't know, actually. There's a fire escape out there…."

He rolled over and pulled her close. "Don't worry about it. I scared him away."

But the operative in him never dismissed any incident as harmless until he'd proven it so. He made a mental note to investigate what was being done to the building and who the construction workers were.

He leaned down and kissed her, then sat back to admire her in the morning light. "You look beautiful."

And she did. He couldn't stop looking at her face, getting to know all her expressions and nuances. He was in deep shit if this was how he remained detached. He was beginning to fear it would be impossible for him to be detached when it came to Ariel. She evoked feelings in him that he hadn't felt in years and she made him question everything. Even things he thought were unquestionable.

In short, she was scaring the hell out of him.

And he couldn't look away.

The sex hadn't hurt. He considered himself a good lover, but with Ariel, he'd suddenly become a bedroom superhero. It was the kind of magic he hadn't experienced often, and he knew better than to take it for granted. Something good had certainly come from her having been with her share of men— she was a spectacular lover.

Like no other woman he'd ever known.

"I hope you don't mind that I stayed all night," he said.

"Of course not." Ariel yawned and stretched,

causing the sheet to fall down to her waist, revealing her small, exquisite breasts.

His gaze dropped to her beautiful brown nipples, which hardened as he watched, and she did nothing to hide herself again, instead lying back on the pillow for him to admire as much as he wanted.

"We sort of crashed out sometime after two,and I didn't mean to just assume I could stay, but—"

"Really, it's fine. Would you like to go get some breakfast? I don't have anything here, but there's a café down the block."

Marc slid his hand across her smooth, warm belly, and his cock stirred. He might have been surprised to be able to perform again so soon, if he hadn't lived through last night and their sexual frenzy.

"I'd rather have you for breakfast," he said.

"Mmm." She rolled onto her side and slid her hand down his belly, then gripped his cock. "Already? I figured you'd need time to recuperate after those three orgasms last night."

"Three? Wow, I only remember two of them."

"I think you lost consciousness at some point," she said, laughing.

"Are you sure I really came three times?"

"I know I did."

Her smile was as intoxicating as her beauty. Marc brushed her hair out of her face and gasped as she began massaging his cock.

"You're relentless," he said. "I've never met any-one like you."

"Surely you've had your share of morning hand jobs," she teased.

"Mostly self-administered, which kills half the fun."

"The hand job is a lost art among women. It's got-ten overshadowed by the ever-popular blow job, but we shouldn't ever dismiss its significance in the bas-tion of male pleasure."

"How about female pleasure?"

"I'm not opposed to being gotten off by hand." She sat up and positioned herself between his legs, where she began using both hands on him.

Marc could only lie back and enjoy. He ad-mired the way her breasts pressed together and swayed as she worked him over, and his cock ached the sweetest kind of ache. She had an amaz-ing skillful touch, aside from the fact that it was just way cool to have a beautiful woman between his legs jerking him off.

"But you prefer other methods?"

She smiled coyly. "Nothing really replaces the dick, though oral comes pretty close."

"Oh?"

She leaned over and took him into her mouth as she continued to work him with her hands, and he lost his ability to form thoughts for a while.

Fifteen minutes later, when she had worked him into a tensed, quivering mass of orgasmic flesh and he was lying against her, gasping as he recovered from the release, he finally had the presence of mind to wonder—what, exactly, would she write about him on her blog?

And how could he justify getting a hand job as a method of undercover investigation? Marc had never found himself questioning his ability to be a good agent before, but now he had to wonder if he even deserved to call himself an operative.

If he was no longer a good operative, what was he, besides a no-good, low-down lying bastard?

Marc sighed and pulled the subject of his so-called investigation closer, so that he could, if nothing else, investigate exactly how she liked to be touched.

If he was going to lose himself, it might as well be in the flesh of a beautiful woman.

"So do we have to, like, walk the cat or anything?"

Marco looked at her as if she'd lost her mind.

"What? I saw someone with a cat on a leash a few times."

"Cats and leashes generally don't get along. Especially not *that* cat, I'd be willing to bet." He nodded at the kitten, who had gotten hold of a sock and was wrestling with it as if its life depended on the sock's defeat.

"As wild as it's acting, I'm surprised it even let me carry it all the way home yesterday."

"She was probably just dehydrated and hungry,

and now that she's had some food and water, she's all energy."

"Remind me again why I brought the little hellion home?"

"She reminds you of yourself?"

"She attacked my foot in the middle of the night. It hurt like hell."

Ariel held her bare leg up so that Marco could see several red scratches across the top of her foot.

"You'll need to take the cat to the vet right away to get her shots and stuff."

"Great. So I probably have some disease now that she broke my skin."

"Hey, I'll take her if you don't want her. Really," he said, and Ariel felt an immediate sense of resolve to keep the cat.

Ridiculous, but true. "No, that's okay." She tried her best to sound grudging. "She seems to like me when she's not attacking me."

"That's what I said about my last girlfriend," Marco said, smiling wryly as he rolled onto his side and covered Ariel's belly with his palm.

They'd been in bed pleasuring each other all morning, and while Ariel was normally opposed to morning-after interactions of any sort, she'd had to make special allowances for Marco, with all his special talents. It was hard not to want him to stick around all day. He'd left her so satisfied last night and this morning that she had started wondering if he'd had some kind of special training in the art of sexual pleasure.

"You weren't a gigolo in a past life, were you?"

He frowned. "No, why?"

"You're just, you know, impressive with your bedroom talents."

"I could say the same thing about you."

"I throw myself into the things I love doing." She sat up and got out of bed to grab some clothes.

"Same here."

Ariel could feel his gaze roaming over her, and turned to put on her panties and bra while facing him. She'd learned long ago to be comfortable naked, because there was nothing sexier than a person at home in their own body.

"I don't suppose shower sex is permitted in that communal bathroom of yours?" he said, his dick growing half-erect again as he watched her.

She looked down at his erection. "You're the most tireless guy I've ever met."

"I have a hard time believing you don't have this effect on every guy you're with."

"To answer your question, no. If you'd taken a look in that shower you wouldn't want to be having sex there, aside from the fact that the other tenants would probably be banging on the door before we finished."

She dug a pair of jeans out of her dresser drawer, along with a black tank top, and put them on, then found her black sandals with the four-inch cork heels and stepped into them.

Marco got out of bed and found his clothes on the

floor, then attempted to wrestle his sock away from the kitten, suffering a few scratches in the process. Ariel sat on the edge of the bed and admired his naked form as he moved, taking in every detail, etching him onto her memory. He may not have been strictly Italian, with his connection to the U.S. and his international accent, but he was most definitely her perfect Italian lover.

But she needed to get her mind off sex long enough to let the poor guy rest up a bit. She didn't want to kill him.

"Any chance you're hungry for breakfast yet? I'm still feeling like a bad host for not having anything to offer you but some lukewarm champagne."

"Sure, just let me wash up a bit and then I'll be ready to grab some food."

He disappeared into the bathroom, and Ariel was tempted to take the opportunity to check her blog, but she didn't want to get busted. He seemed a little too suspicious of her frequent "e-mail checking." She'd gotten a chance to post last night after he'd fallen asleep, when she'd slipped out into the hallway with her computer, but now she decided not to risk it. Instead, she used the sink in her room to wash up, brushed her teeth and pulled her hair back into a sleek ponytail, then applied a tiny bit of makeup to keep from looking as though she'd stayed up most of the night screwing some guy's brains out.

Marco came back just as she was feeding the cat.

Once the little fur ball was occupied, they left the apartment in search of sustenance for themselves.

Ariel's neighborhood café bustled with Saturday-morning activity, and already she recognized half the faces there—the late-morning crowd, as she had come to think of them. They picked an outdoor table and sat down, and she found herself wondering if Marco would be the first of a series of men she brought here, or the only one.

The Only One was not a label she frequently put on men, but lovers of special talent deserved unique designations, right?

A waiter came and took their coffee and pastry orders. When he was gone, Marco cast a curious glance at Ariel. "You've gotten awfully quiet since we left the apartment. What's bothering you?"

"Nothing," she said.

It occurred to her now that his English had gotten more casual since their first meeting. He'd gone from sounding like the typical English-as-a-second-language speaker, formal and perhaps a bit stilted, to sounding like a typical American. She wasn't sure whether to mention it or keep the observation to herself, so she erred on the side of caution.

It was the sort of thing only a linguist would notice anyway. She'd majored in linguistics in college and all it had seemed to do for her was give her the annoying habit of noticing the nuances of people's speech patterns, which rarely got her a job.

"You're sure it's nothing?"

Ariel shrugged. "Sorry. I guess I'm just feeling a little weirded out that we've gone from meeting in front of the embassy to having breakfast like a couple in the space of twenty-four hours."

"Are you used to moving more slowly?"

"I just like to define things up front so neither of us have the wrong expectations, you know?"

Marco frowned. "I thought we kind of did that already."

"Well, I know you want us to do the getting-to-know-each-other thing, and that's cool."

"But?"

"I feel like I should come with a disclaimer tattooed on my ass or something—Not Into Heavy Involvement."

"So you basically want to make sure I know you're only interested in me as a sex object?"

"'Sex object' sounds so cold and heartless," she said, smiling as the waiter dropped off their coffee and croissants. "I prefer 'sex toy' or perhaps 'sex buddy.'"

"How about 'booty call guy.'"

"Sure, that works if you want to go all hip-hop influenced."

"And what makes you think I'd be interested in such crass objectification?"

"You're a guy?"

"Hey, that's not fair. Guys have feelings not connected to our dicks, you know."

"I'm sorry, you're right. I'm being utterly crass.

It's hard not to get that way after a decade or so of dating."

"I should know. I've got a decade's head start on you."

"Any long-term relationships to speak of?"

He made a face that was an odd mixture of chagrined and blasé. "Depends on what you mean by long-term. I've been with a few women for more than a year."

"I call anything longer than a month long-term."

"You might be an extreme example of commitment-phobia, though. I'm not sure I've met any women as skittish about the subject as you are."

And he probably had never met a woman with parents as screwed up as hers had been, either. When the primary example of love in her life had been between a pair of people so selfish and irresponsible they couldn't be bothered to take care of their own children, she didn't think it was illogical that she had chosen to run in the opposite direction of everything that reminded her of them—including commitment.

"I'm not skittish. I just know what I like."

"And it's casual sex?"

"Not exactly. I just like to avoid unmet expectations. And if your longest relationship has been a couple of years, I'd say we're probably both the type that likes to keep things from getting too heavy."

Marco shrugged. "You're right. I've never stuck around past when most relationships naturally hit a rough patch."

"Right. I say, why stick around when it's not fun anymore?"

He sipped his coffee. And Ariel suddenly got the odd feeling she was being talked into a trap.

"What if it kept being fun past the usual expiration date? Then what would you do?"

"It never does."

"But what if?"

"I guess I'd stick around. Hypothetically, I mean." But she knew that kind of thing just didn't happen.

She'd seen long-term relationships. They all sucked.

"Call me a romantic fool, but I do at least believe it's possible that two people could stay happy together."

"Okay," she said, smiling into her coffee cup. "You're a romantic fool."

"But all teasing aside," Marco said, and Ariel found herself wondering again if he had anything to hide, if his mysterious accent was a hint of something he wasn't willing to admit. "I totally agree with you that it's important to be honest about what we want in a relationship up front."

"Good." And she was about to start in on her standard I'm-just-looking-for-sex spiel when it struck her that she didn't really feel like saying it to Marco. Maybe it was all his pie-in-the-sky talk that had her feeling odd.

Maybe.

Or maybe it was the fact that for the first time in

months she'd woken up feeling truly not-depressed. Like even, perhaps, happy again.

Amazing what a night of really great sex could do for a girl.

"I'm looking for someone I can hang out with, have great sex with and get to know—for as long as we're both enjoying ourselves," Marco continued.

Ariel set down her coffee cup and poked at her croissant. "I guess that's okay." She sounded lame even to her own ears. "I mean, I'm cool with being friends, so long as we both understand that the relationship isn't going anywhere permanent."

Marco looked at her then at her croissant, which she was now breaking into little pieces. "Sure," he replied.

"I'm not even going to be in Italy for very long. I'm planning to move back to the U.S. in the fall."

"Right. So it sounds like we've reached an understanding."

Right. Whew. Good to have that out of the way.

But something felt as if it had been left unspoken, or unaccounted for or something. Didn't they need to address the fact that they'd just had the most amazing sex ever?

And where was there to go after having had the best sex of one's life? Would any other lover ever be able to measure up? Or, when the fun had ended with Marco, was she doomed to live a life of searching for but never quite finding that perfect lover again?

Even worse, what if sex this good was addictive? She was pretty damn sure it could be.

Addiction. The very word made her nauseous.

Aside from the regular consumption of coffee, Ariel had spent her life avoiding anything that might be addictive, after having seen what addiction had done to her parents and had nearly done to her brother.

She'd have to tread carefully here, and be sure to get out fast if she began feeling that Marco wasn't a thing she could let go of whenever she chose. Some people might accuse her of confusing emotional attachment with addiction, but she knew the truth. She knew that both could cause the sort of pain that destroyed lives.

8

Making the Rules—And Then Breaking Them

I've never been good at following relationship rules. I believe we've established that sad little fact over and over again here on the blog. But what about the rules we make for ourselves? Our own personal sex codes of conduct? Are we allowed to break those rules with repercussions?

I know, I know, what you all really want to know is, how did the first date go? You're just a bunch of nosy blog readers waiting to be fed your daily dose of titillation, right?

Right. Well. Anyway. The first night with X was, undoubtedly, amazing. I will have to spoon-feed you the details, though, because I've got something more urgent on my mind.

I was explaining to X my expectations for a romantic relationship, or perhaps my relative lack of them, and I found myself wondering if I was breaking my own rules by agreeing to his. He wants to get to know me—like, you know, really get to know me.

And I agreed to play along. Maybe it just makes him feel less like an asshole than if he were to just sleep with me and let that be the whole of the relationship. Maybe he can't be honest with himself about the state of postmodern male-female relationships.

Or am I just being cynical? Is it possible that I'm the only one looking for sex without the strings attached?

Comments:

1. juju says: My # 1 relationship rule is, no sleeping over. Can't have no woman waking up looking all scary the next morning beside me.

2. Asiana says: juju, you're a real catch, you know that?

3. joe cool says: Since when is there a such thing as the "postmodern relationship?"

4. Mia says: Since we, um, you know, entered the postmodern era?

5. AllenD says: Eurogirl, it's cruel of you to make us wait for the details.

6. Eurogirl says: I won't hold out on you much longer. Let's just say it was such a good first time, I'm at a loss to adequately describe it.

7. joe cool says: If it's so good, why are you worried about him wanting to get to know you? Are you like the most commitment phobic woman on earth or what?

8. Eurogirl says: Yes. I am. And since when is that a bad thing?

ARIEL WOKE UP TO the morning sun glaring in her window, along with the dark form of a figure. For a moment she was frozen and silent with terror, thinking of how she'd imagined spotting Kostas on the sidewalk. He'd tracked her down, and he was here now to kill her, or to torture her first, then kill her.

But when her brain slowed down enough to process the scene, she realized she was looking at a hairy mustached man on a ladder. Not Kostas. One of his colleagues, perhaps?

She screeched and tugged the covers up to hide herself, then cursed the fact that she hadn't yet put up curtains.

Then she noticed the hard hat, and remembered how Marco had insisted a construction worker had been outside her window Saturday morning, as well. It was probably time to ask the landlord about the issue.

She yelled "go away" in Italian—one of the first phrases she'd learned—and the man moved on up the ladder. Ariel took advantage of the moment's privacy, once she was sure he was gone, to dive out of bed and dress in a hurry.

It was Monday morning, and Marco had gone back to his place the night before to get ready for work the next day. Ariel, too, had to get ready for her first day of tutoring, but she didn't start until afternoon when the kids got home from school.

Once she'd gotten her clothes on and gone down the hallway to the bathroom she went about making her bed and feeding that cat.

The extremely noisy cat, that had kept her up half the night yowling and scratching at things. But the little fur ball also knew how to use its cuteness to its own advantage and had curled up purring against Ariel at various times during the night to sleep for a short while before going on another rampage. And the way she looked up at Ariel, blinking sweetly, then butted her head against her when she wanted attention, was kind of adorable.

She needed to pick a name for the damn cat, too. She couldn't keep calling it "cat."

Someone knocked at the door, and she opened it to find her landlady Fabiana Medici.

"I tell you men working on roof, yes?"

"I saw one of them," Ariel said. "He was staring in my window today and a few days ago." She spoke slowly and used hand gestures for "staring" and "window," which she knew from tutoring rarely helped much, but when she spoke to Fabiana she found herself always doing it anyway.

Her landlord scowled at the window in reproach. "I tell him no look in window, okay?"

Ariel nodded. "Yes, thank you. I would appreciate that."

The cat chose that moment to dart out from under the bed and skid across the floor to her food bowl. When she saw that it contained what was apparently the wrong flavor of food, she looked up at Ariel and yowled.

"You have cat!" Fabiana said, and Ariel tried to guess whether that was a good or bad thing.

Her landlord caught the worried look and assured Ariel, "Is okay. I love cats!"

"Oh, good. I'm sorry I didn't ask first."

"No, no. You travel, or you go away for night, you tell me and I feed cat for you, okay?"

Ariel expelled a sigh of relief. She was actually growing attached to the annoying little thing and dreaded the idea of having to give it away. Who else would put up with its wildness? She identified with the cat's untamed nature, though she was probably reading way too much into its affectionate blinks and head butts in thinking it recognized a kindred spirit in her, too.

"Thank you. Actually," she said on a whim, "I may occasionally be staying at a friend's apartment, so I might take you up on that some time."

Was she really already planning for overnights at Marco's place? After a weekend as intensely sexual as they'd had, she could only hope for more of the same, and Marco, for his part, seemed just as interested in continuing what they'd started as she was.

Fabiana frowned and nodded. "Yes, I check on cat every night."

Ariel thought of correcting the woman, but she didn't feel like trying to explain the nuances of their misunderstanding. Fabiana would probably figure out on her own that it wouldn't be a good idea to just stop in any old time to check on the cat. Or at least Ariel hoped she would. She'd learned from renting throughout Europe that landlords and tenants were much more casual about personal space than Americans tended to be.

She said goodbye to Fabiana and closed the door. Inside her little room, she was actually starting to feel kind of at home. Or at least the cat made it feel sort of homey.

The no-name cat. She thought of her brother then, of how he'd have already given the cat a name and probably bought it a different-colored collar for each day of the week, along with various cat furniture and little ceramic cat bowls with pictures of fish or something on them.

She hadn't talked to Trey in a few days now, so she counted back the hours to make sure it was an okay time to call. Nine hours earlier on the West Coast of the U.S. meant it was midnight there, but he wouldn't be in bed yet since he was a night owl.

Ariel dug her mobile phone out of her purse and dialed his number, then went to the couch to sit—

The couch owned by Fabiana that had now been shredded on one corner. As she inspected the damage inflicted by tiny claws, her brother answered the phone.

"Do you know how to make a cat stop scratching stuff?" she asked him as a greeting.

"Hey, sis. A cat? Did you get a cat?"

"Um, sort of. I mean, I found this stray, and it took a liking to me and I kind of brought it home, but now it's taking over my life or something."

"Ariel, I'm proud of you. A cat is a big commitment for a girl who spends her life drifting around the globe."

"I don't know what I was thinking."

"Maybe you were thinking like a normal person for once—feeling that you'd like to have something permanent in your life to love?"

"Hey, I've got you. You're pretty permanent."

"Yeah, but I'm not going to let you pet me or sleep with me."

"This kitten's kind of wild. It doesn't let me pet it or sleep with it, either."

"Sounds like the perfect animal for you. You're pretty undomesticated, too, you know."

Ariel smiled as she watched the cat glare at her, apparently waiting for a more acceptable breakfast. Maybe that was what she'd liked about it—that it was untamed, detached from domestic life.

She tucked the phone between her ear and shoul-

der and got up to feed the cat *again,* as she continued talking.

"So any tips to keep it from shredding the furniture?"

"Give it a toy to play with. I've also heard of
shooting it with a water gun every time it starts
scratching something."

"That seems pretty cruel."

"You could trim its claws a bit to keep them from
being too sharp. Then they can't do so much damage."

"That sounds dangerous," she said, eyeing the
scratches on her feet that the cat had already put there.

"Maybe the vet will do it for you."

Right. The vet. She needed to find one and take
the cat there today.

"Okay, next problem. I need a name for it."

"Liberace?"

"No."

"How about something Italian? Julius Caesar?"

"It's a girl cat."

"Angelica?"

"She hasn't demonstrated any angelic qualities
so far."

"Then that's the perfect name for her."

"It's too long. I can't call 'Angelica' every time
I'm looking for the cat." But as soon as she said the
name, the cat let out a long, high-pitched yowl.

"I heard that," Trey said. "She likes the name.
Go with it."

Ariel plopped some more foul-smelling cat food

into her dish and winced at the sight of it. Definitely a downside of having a cat in a studio apartment was having to live with the smell of this crap all the time. "She's yowling because I'm getting her food right now."

"Angelica Turner. It's perfect," Trey went on. "She needs a middle name, too…"

"No, she doesn't. She's a cat. She's not going to have a social security number or a passport or anything that would require her to give her birth name. She doesn't need a middle name."

"Angelica…Carina. That means sweetie pie in Italian, doesn't it?"

"How the hell would I know? Do I sound like the kind of person who goes around calling anyone sweetie pie?"

"Angelica Carina Turner. It's perfect." Trey's voice had taken on a dreamy quality, as if he was naming his first child or something.

Next thing she knew, he'd be sending her little knitted cat sweaters in the mail.

"Cats don't wear sweaters, you know," she said.

"What are you talking about?"

"Oh, nothing." She stared at the kitten, who was greedily eating its nasty-smelling food.

Angelica Carina. Great, she had a cat with a porn star name.

Ariel went to the window, now free of roof workers, and opened it to air the place out, then flopped down on the couch as Trey started in on his report of the latest wedding-planning news.

When he ran out of air, Ariel inserted an "Mmm-hmm" to let him know she was listening. But in truth, she had a hard time caring whether his wedding invitations were printed on white or cream parchment paper, or whatever the hell he was talking about.

She loved her brother, but he could be a wee bit obsessive about the details.

"You're not listening to me," she heard him say. "What's going on?"

"Nothing," she lied.

"I saw your blog. Who's this X guy you keep waxing rhapsodic about?"

Ariel tried not to get creeped out that her brother was reading her blog, but still, she regretted ever having let him in on how she'd gotten a book deal without having written a book.

"Just another guy. No one special."

That, too, felt like a lie.

She got a sick feeling in her gut. Maybe she couldn't take on a boyfriend *and* a cat at the same time.

"Then why do you have that weird tone in your voice, like you're about to throw up?"

"Because it's a really bad time to meet someone I actually like."

"Right. It's awful to fall in love. It's pure hell. Much better to be alone."

"Shut up. You're just all starry-eyed because you

found Mr. Perfect and you're in the middle of planning your wedding."

"What? You think it's easy planning a wedding? It's a real test of a relationship, let me tell you. I think that's why weddings exist—to make the people who aren't that serious give up and call the whole thing off."

"I'm only planning to be here until the end of summer, and then I'm coming back to the U.S. for your wedding."

"That doesn't mean you have to stay here for good, you know."

It wasn't like Ariel to make such long-term plans, or to stick with any plans she had made, but while a terrorist threat had only made her flee a country, somehow, the threat of true love made her want to flee the entire continent.

So she had a few issues. Didn't everyone?

"I'm not dealing with the jet lag. If I fly all the way back to California, and then Hawaii, I'm staying for good."

She was planning to arrive in San Francisco two weeks before the wedding to help Trey with last-minute preparations, and then they'd fly on to Hawaii for the wedding itself.

"For a world traveler, you're really weird about jet lag."

"I don't deal well with sleep interruptions." She was aware how much her reasons were sounding like lame excuses.

"Tell me about this X guy. Who is he? What does he do?"

"He works at the U.S. Embassy here, doing security stuff."

"You mean like a James Bond type?"

"No," Ariel said. "Just a security guard."

"You sounded pretty hot for him on your blog. Like, totally in heat."

"I didn't realize how much I was gushing. Is it really that bad?"

"Yes, dear. It is."

"Yikes. I guess I need to cool it."

"It's actually a refreshing change to hear you sounding less jaded and more like a schoolgirl with a huge crush."

"I don't sound jaded usually."

"Honey, jaded should be your middle name."

"So what's wrong with being jaded?"

Ariel bit her lip, watching the cat—no, make that Angelica—clean itself after its meal. She didn't often consider how her casual attitude about sex might come across to the people she cared about.

"After a while, sex starts feeling like various arrangements of body parts if you don't insert some emotion into the act."

She wanted to protest, but she was afraid her little brother was right. Various arrangements of body parts, indeed. That was exactly how sex had started feeling to her—before she'd met Marco.

Had the problem really been a lack of emotional connection to any of her recent partners?

"Hello? You still there?" Trey asked.

"Yeah, I'm here. I was just thinking about what you said. I think you gave me my next blog topic."

"Ooh, do I get credit?"

"I'll call you a 'dear friend,' okay?"

He sighed. "Why not 'my flaming gay brother, Trey Turner?'"

"Oh, you know, because it's an anonymous blog and I don't want weirdos figuring out my real identity and stalking me."

Ariel caught a movement out of the corner of her eye. She looked over at the window and saw the mustached man climbing down the fire escape. She glared, and he quickly moved on.

"Speaking of weirdos, what's up with that anonymous poster on your blog? Does that guy really know who you are?"

"I was hoping not too many people had seen his posts. But I guess it's possible he does. He could have hacked my blog somehow."

"Do you know who it is? How does he know your name?"

"I think it's Kostas, the guy I was last dating in Greece." Ariel fervently hoped Kostas was in the hands of the Greek authorities, but thought it wise to remind her brother of his name in case she hadn't imagined seeing him.

"Oh, Mr. Hairy Ass?"

"Yeah," Ariel said, not thinking it smart to explain the whole story over the phone.

"How could you date someone with a coat of fur on their ass? That would be a deal breaker for me."

"You spend a lot more time looking at guys' asses than I do."

"That's true. Anyway, he could have gotten a wax job or something."

"Straight Greek men don't wax. That's pretty much an American metrosexual phenomenon."

"God, you did *not* just say metrosexual. That term is so five years ago."

"I've been out of the U.S. for five years. I've lost touch with what all the urban men there are doing these days."

"The latest thing is full body waxing."

"The pubic hair, too?"

"Yeah, for that streamlined, aerodynamic look."

"Eww, that's bad. Do any women really like that?"

"Apparently, some do."

"You're not waxed down there, are you?"

"Do you really want to know?"

"No, you're right. I don't."

"I'll just say this. It's hell on the balls."

Ariel groaned. Definitely not a visual of her little brother that she wanted.

He continued on about the prewedding spa treatment he was planning to do, and Ariel leaned back on the couch and listened. Trey was, at the very least, a pleasant distraction from the bigger issues in her life. Like Angelica, the kitten from hell, and the guy she didn't want to be falling for and her growing paranoia that her terrorist ex-boyfriend was possibly trying to hunt her down.

She wasn't sure how her life had gotten so complicated all of a sudden, but she was pretty sure she had no one but herself to blame for the complications. As if to punctuate that thought, the cat darted across the room and for no apparent reason attacked Ariel's big toe.

9

Various Arrangements of Body Parts

One of the dangers of a hyperactive sex life, a dear friend pointed out to me recently, is that it's easy to get jaded about it all. Insert body part A into body part B, massage body part C, while kissing body part D and so on.

When you find yourself going through the motions and no longer feeling like your aim in life is simply the pursuit of physical pleasure, what do you do then?

Retreat to a mountaintop to meditate on the problem? Turn to booze? Become celibate?

Or do you look for something more in your romantic relationships?

I'll admit, I've spent most of my life avoiding that whole category known to some as "something more," and known to others as "love" and "commitment" and stuff like that.

I'll spare you the self-psychoanalysis, but let's just say addiction runs in my family, and the last thing I need is to get addicted, especially to a person or a relationship.

But the other day my friend makes this observation, and it was like, duh, why didn't I think of that. I'd been suffering from the "various arrangements of body parts" syndrome for months, and suddenly I meet this guy—X, in case you haven't been paying attention—and things are humming right along again.

My sex life has improved a hundred percent, and I would like to credit it all to X's bedroom skills, which as you all know are impressive, but I'm afraid I have to admit, it's something more. It's a connection that goes beyond the physical.

A connection that involves the emotions and the intellect, as well as the body, supposedly makes for the best kind of sex, but since I go around avoiding such things, I don't get to experience it often. Therein lies the dilemma for commitment-phobes like me—how do you keep having great sex without risking getting involved in something addictive?

Can you have the deeper connections without the complications? I don't think so.

Which means, basically, that I'm freaking out. What do I do with my commitment phobias? Do I let go of them in pursuit of the best sex life has to offer?

I guess most people just close their eyes and dive in and hope for the best. I guess you'll all probably tell me that's what I'm supposed to do.

But honestly, I don't even know if X is feeling what I'm feeling, and if he isn't, then what?

I hear all your little fingers itching to type "coward, coward." Name call if you will, but it's a delicate balance, having a guy I don't want to scare away but also don't want to get too close. It's one of the disadvantages of living and loving temporarily in Europe—if I don't intend to stay, I have to avoid long-term commitments.

That's my story anyway. I just haven't managed to convince my heart or my body that temporary is still the way to go.

Comments:

1. lolo says: You are so right. The whole easy sex thing gets tired after a while.

2. TinaLee says: I stopped arranging body parts for sport years ago and haven't once missed it. It's no fun unless there are some real feelings involved. And it sounds like you might be confusing love with addiction.

3. Jimmycap says: Whoa. I thought the point of this blog was about various arrangements of body parts.

4. Eurogirl says: I know. Scary stuff when I start questioning my whole purpose in life.

5. hillaryB says: Love sucks. Don't let it fool you.

6. Obaby says: This is the most jaded blog I've ever seen. I think you totally need to soften up and get some love in your life.

7. Anonymous says: Love can get you into big trouble, you know. You'd better watch out.

ARIEL COULDN'T DECIDE whether to delete the anonymous comment. She'd better watch out? She glanced around nervously, as if there was some danger right there in the same room with her. She was being ridiculous. The post may have been from the anonymous poster who'd left the previous disturbing comments, but this one was a bit more ambiguous. It didn't address her by name and it potentially could have been from anyone.

But her blog prompted people to choose a user name before posting, and ninety-nine percent of her readers did, simply because one had to actually type in the name "Anonymous" to post anonymously. In reality, anyone could post anonymously because leaving an e-mail address with the user name was optional. Some people even posted under multiple names just so they could say something a little out of character using a different identity on occasion.

Ariel didn't care, so long as people felt comfortable participating. But since Anonymous had started leaving comments last week, her blog activity had died down significantly, and she didn't think it was a coincidence.

She selected the anonymous comment and hit Delete. Whether it was from the same person or not, it wasn't going to help to leave it there scaring away more readers, screwing up the vibe on her blog.

Ariel dug around in her wardrobe until she found the bag she used for tutoring, then spent some time going through it to prepare for her first day of work. She chose an appropriately modest outfit to wear on the job and got herself ready to go.

First day back among the gainfully employed, and she was already feeling a little sad to lose her endless free time. Sure, the paycheck would be most welcome, but there was nothing quite like having a week uninterrupted by work spread out before her.

Ariel glanced at her watch once she was all done, wondering if Marco was at his job now. He must have been. He hadn't told her his work hours exactly, but she figured it wouldn't be a good time to call and say hi. Instead, she decided to text message him.

She got out her phone, started a new message and typed in, Miss u. How's it going? I'm off 2 work soon. Can't wait 2 do u 2night.

Then she hit Send. A few minutes later, her phone beeped with notice that she had a new message. It was from Marco. Miss u 2. Want 2 meet 4 lunch 2day?

Ariel smiled. And she got sick to her stomach all over again. What the hell was wrong with her? Why couldn't she just relax and enjoy herself when a great guy wanted to spend his every waking hour with her?

She keyed in the words, Yes, call me when u can, and hit Send. Then she immediately regretted it.

Maybe she needed to back off, to make sure Marco understood where she was coming from. Maybe the sick feeling in her gut was really her instincts telling her this was all wrong, that if he was coming on so strong, so fast, he had to have an ulterior motive.

She dropped her phone in her purse and decided to get the hell out of her apartment. No sense in sitting around here feeling claustrophobic and uneasy when she had all of Rome at her fingertips.

She needed to decide how to handle Marco, and she needed to decide fast.

ARIEL FLIPPED ON the lamp by the door of her apartment and yawned as she dropped her bag on top of a bookshelf. A lunchtime rendezvous with Marco, followed by a first day of tutoring that had been a little grueling considering the vastly different ages and ability levels of the three kids in the family, had left her exhausted and ready to enjoy a night at home alone.

She kicked off her heels and turned around, then stopped cold in her tracks at the sight of Kostas sitting on her couch.

A little strangled scream escaped her throat, and she felt as if a weight had been dropped on her chest.

He held a gun pointed straight at her.

"Ariel," he said. "You should have been expecting me."

"How did you get in?" she asked lamely, but the open window revealed the answer. Anyone who wanted in simply had to climb the fire escape.

"Better to ask why, not how."

"Why?" she whispered.

"Tell me what you know."

"I don't know anything." She took a step back, but he aimed the gun at her heart then, and she froze again.

"Come sit," he said, nodding at the chair next to the couch.

Ariel complied slowly, inching her way across the floor to the chair. She had never faced death before. She'd never been so close to a gun, let alone had one pointed at her. She wished she could have been more dignified about it, but she just wanted to cry and beg for her life.

Instead, she focused on breathing. In and out, in and out.

"You are lying," Kostas said, resting the hand with the gun pointed at her on his knee now. "You disappeared from Athens without even saying goodbye, then the police came looking for me."

Ariel tried to play dumb. "Why would the police be looking for you? Is that why you have a gun?"

"You discovered things you shouldn't have."

"I don't know what you're talking about," she lied again.

"Ariel, my darling, there are ways I can get the

information from you, whether you want to tell me or not."

She stopped breathing, stopped thinking.

"It would pain me to torture you, since I think you are such a lovely girl, but I would do it. I have hurt people I loved before."

"I'm sorry I left without saying goodbye," she said, her desperate brain grasping for a way out. "I was planning to leave Greece for a job in Rome and I didn't have the heart to tell you. I thought it would be easier if I just disappeared."

"I don't believe you."

"Kostas, it's the truth! I was a coward, that's all. I've never been good at breakups, and I'm ashamed to say you're not the first guy I've just skipped town on. It's kind of my MO."

"Your *what?*"

"Oh, sorry, that's an American term. It just means that it's what I do."

He stood up abruptly, and Ariel's breath caught in her throat. "That's enough of your lies."

Kostas jammed the barrel of the gun into the tender spot between her jaw and neck. "If I shoot you now, the bullet will travel up into your brain and you will die instantly."

Ariel opened her mouth to speak, but no sounds would come out. Then she heard a miraculous noise, a key being inserted into her door and turned.

Kostas heard it, too, and they both stared at the

front door for a split second before he sprang toward the open window and climbed out.

A moment later, Ariel was staring at Fabiana, who blinked at her, confused.

"*Ariella,* you no be here?" she said in her broken English.

Ariel jumped up from the chair and hurried to the window, then slammed it shut and locked it. She could not see Kostas down below, and she could only hope he was gone for the time being. She turned to her landlord and heaved a huge sigh of relief.

Fabiana gave her a perplexed look for being in such a hurry to close the window.

"You no hot?"

It was miserably hot inside the apartment, but Ariel wouldn't be leaving the window open again anytime soon.

"Actually, there was just a man inside my apartment. You scared him away."

Fabiana's eyes widened. "A thief here?"

Ariel nodded. "Yes, maybe. He had a gun and he was here when I came home a few minutes ago, but when you opened the door you scared him away."

"I call the *Carabinieri* for you now!"

"No, it's okay. I'll do it. I will need to describe him."

Fabiana nodded. "You want me stay with you? I just come here to check on your cat, but I stay here, or you come to my apartment?"

"No, I'll go to a friend's house after I talk to the police."

But Ariel knew the Italian police would be no help at all. This whole Kostas thing was her big hint to go back to the U.S. now, before it was too late. But until she could arrange her ticket her only hope was to enlist Marco's help since he knew about security and probably had access to a gun.

Her landlord cast her a worried look, but nodded and backed out of the apartment. "I be watching out for you, okay?"

"Yes, thank you." Ariel smiled and nodded, then waved as the older woman closed the door. A second later the lock clicked into place, and she wondered for the first time about Angelica.

"Here, kitty-kitty," she called, suddenly terrified that the cat might be hurt.

She knelt and peered under the couch, then the bed. From behind the wardrobe, she heard a familiar yowl.

"Hey, you," she said as the cat came lurching out from its hiding spot. "I made a vet appointment for you for tomorrow, but luckily for you, we'll probably have to skip it."

Angelica bumped her head against Ariel's leg and purred, finally showing a little affection. She rubbed the kitten's back, but it didn't ease her fear that somewhere out there, Kostas was lurking. Waiting for his chance to get to her again.

She would have to play with the cat later. Right now, she needed to talk to Marco. She found her phone and dialed his number, which she already knew by heart.

10

How to Say Sex in Italian

I've never considered myself a racist. I mean, I'm pretty much an equal opportunity lover. I've been with men of every race, nationality, blah blah blah. My bedroom has been a virtual United Nations of lovers.

But there's just something about Italian men. Dare I say I have a bias in favor of them above all the other men on earth?

Okay, I'll say it. Italian guys rock.

To be fair to all the other men of the planet, I'll point out some of the failings of Italian men first. I mean, yeah, they have a tendency to be Mama's Boys in the worst kind of way. Forty-year-olds living with their mothers, anyone? Ick.

And sure, they can be utter and complete sexists, and impossibly lecherous and let's don't even mention the Madonna-Whore Complex so many of them seem to suffer from.

But when you find a good one, oh, honey, have you found a good one.

Let's take my latest lover, for example, the one we're calling X to protect the identities of the hot and sexy.

X has all the right moves. He knows how to treat a girl like a goddess and he knows the meaning of the word *romance*. I'm sure I don't have to point out to you how rare these two qualities are. Let alone the fact that he's hot as hell and has an accent that makes my panties wet.

But more important is that incredible stroke of genetic luck that makes him a guy with the most exquisite cock I've ever seen. You'll have to excuse me if I get a little fancy with the adjectives here.

Perfectly shaped, with a firm shaft and a smooth, beautiful head, I could spend all day getting to know it intimately. Believe me, I've tried. For three hours!

But the pleasure I experience with my mouth on him is nothing compared to what he can do inside me. If it didn't make me sound like such a dork, I might confess to shedding a few tears of joy at what it's like to screw him....

Comments:

1. Skywalker says: I wish someone would wax poetic about my dick.

2. TiaMaria says: Most men seem to do a good enough job of that themselves.

3. Hummer says: Women who give three-hour blow jobs should be elected president of the universe.

4. Eurogirl says: I don't think I can handle that kind of responsibility.

5. CKCKCK says: Especially if you're busy giving three-hour blow jobs.

6. nuguy says: we're all going to develop complexes if your sex life keeps being this much better than ours.

7. B cool says: Yeah. Nobody likes a bragger.

8. dharmachick says: I would fall asleep if I spent that much time down there.

MARC SHOULD HAVE stopped reading Ariel's blog by now. He knew that. But he couldn't. It had become a compulsion. And it had sent him off the deep end, confusing his investigative work with his personal life.

His dumb dick was throbbing after having read Ariel's latest post about him, and he sat there staring at the computer screen.

What if he posted a comment of his own? Just one little comment.

Nothing serious, nothing that would reveal his identity.

Just something light and breezy.

It felt weird to consider crossing the line from secret, anonymous reader to active participant on the blog. He'd felt that way every time he'd ever posted to a public forum on the Internet. It conflicted with his natural tendency to be the watcher, the secret observer. Besides, he was the guy she was writing about, and what would he say, anyway? *Hey, that X guy's pretty damn lucky!*

That was self-evident.

And yet…he hated feeling left out of the party.

Marc clicked the Post a Comment button and typed into the Name field "Marco Polo." Then he erased it. Then he typed it again. He kind of liked the idea of making Ariel a little paranoid about whether it was him reading the blog. She might never make the connection, but after the last time he'd walked in on her blogging, she could start to suspect he was on to her.

But why even let her suspect anything? Wasn't it always better to hold on to any possible advantage in every situation?

The fact that he would even risk revealing his hand was out of character for him, when such sloppiness could get him killed in his line of work. That he sort of *wanted* Ariel to find out was even more disturbing. He'd never felt that was about anyone. It meant putting himself at risk…but for what?

He was beginning to see more than ever the peril of mixing his work with his personal life. It left him confused about where Marc the spy stopped and

Marc the guy began. Or were they one and the same? And if they were, why did Ariel make him feel as if he was splitting in two?

Part of him figured they'd be breaking up soon enough and it wouldn't matter anyway. And some perverse part of him figured his knowledge of her blog identity needed to be revealed at just the right time, to serve as a mercy killing of their doomed relationship.

He thought of his ex-girlfriend, and the angry text messages and the scene in the embassy lobby. He totally deserved her wrath, and the wrath of quite a few other women. He was an asshole.

He tabbed to the message field and started typing.

X is a lucky guy. Incredibly lucky.

Then he clicked the Post button, and a few seconds later, his dumb comment appeared at the bottom of the list.

Marc spun around in the desk chair and surveyed his lifeless apartment, feeling a wave of existential angst settling over him. There wasn't even a plant to liven things up. He'd taken the place for its view of the Roman skyline and its proximity to the embassy. The sad thing was it felt as much like home— or as little—as anywhere he'd ever lived.

He would be leaving it behind, too. With the lack of leads on the supposed terrorist threat at the embassy, his assignment would soon be finished. At least, if he had anything to do with it, he'd be moving on to something new before long.

And for the first time since childhood, he felt a sense of longing for a permanent place to call home. And a person to care if he was there or not. If he died now, no one would even give a crap.

God, he was starting to sound like a bad made-for-TV movie—CIA op facing his own mortality gets pangs of homesickness and feelings of malaise about ever-changing lifestyle.

The ticking clock on the wall said he still had five hours before Ariel would be free to see him again. He was lonely. He wanted to talk to someone. He wanted to get the hell outside of his own head.

He thought of his old mentor Nicholas Kozowski, who had been like a father to him since his first years in the CIA. In a world where no one could trust anyone, Nicholas had been trustworthy. The older man had been there for him in his early days as an operative, and given him a gruff but reliable emotional support network that he'd never experienced before. Marc trusted him more than he did his own distant, money-obsessed father, who had proven over the years to be reliable at providing private school tuition and not much of anything else.

He hadn't talked to Nicholas in too long. He picked up the phone and dialed the number he knew by heart before he could change his mind.

There was no answer, and then a voice mail recording with Nicholas's voice invited him to try calling his cell phone instead. Marc jotted that number on a piece of paper, then hung up and dialed again.

After a couple of rings, Nicholas answered with a gruff hello.

"I thought you'd be retired and gone to Tahiti by now," Marc said by way of greeting.

"Marc? How the hell are you?" Nicholas's wry smile came through in his voice, and Marc felt inordinately relieved to know that someone in the world was happy to hear from him.

"Pretty good, man," he lied. "Just wondering the same about you."

Nicholas sighed noisily. "You call me up after three years just to ask me how I'm doing?"

"God, has it been that long?"

"Not since we were in Naples for that overnight mission."

So now he had "lousy friend" to add to his list of reasons why he was an asshole. Perfect.

"What's really going on?"

"I was just wondering if you were going to be in Italy anytime soon."

"It's funny you mention it, because I'll be in Rome next week."

"So let's get together when you're in town. Go out for drinks, maybe?"

"Sure thing, Marc. I'll drop you a line when I get there."

They said their goodbyes and hung up. Marc

found himself alone again at his desk, staring at the computer, feeling like an utter and complete jackass.

Great sex with a beautiful woman who wasn't into forming attachments wasn't a bad thing. He should have been thrilled, right?

But he was feeling guilty as hell about the whole thing. Which was unlike him.

He liked Ariel. A lot. And he was enjoying their time together more than he'd enjoyed anything in a long time.

So what was the problem?

He was lying to her. And no longer for a good reason. A weekend of checking her out had convinced him she was simply a girl who'd bumbled into a relationship with a terrorist unintentionally. Now that he knew he didn't need to further investigate her, how could he continue a relationship that had started on false pretenses without letting her know what had really been going on?

Reading what she'd posted on her blog over the weekend hadn't helped his conscience. Not to mention reading what she'd posted about previous guys. It was completely weird, having such insight into her sex life and her private thoughts, when she didn't even know his real name.

His phone rang, and Marc startled at the sound. When he saw that it was Ariel's number, his morose mood instantly disappeared.

"Hey," he answered.

"I need your help," Ariel said. "Can you come over?"

"What's wrong?"

He listened as she described what had just happened to her moments before, and how she'd stumbled onto her ex-boyfriend's terrorist activities, and his gut clenched.

He couldn't handle the thought of Ariel having had a gun pressed to her neck while he'd been sitting here on his ass doing nothing. The thought of her alone and in such danger made him furious and inordinately afraid of what might have happened.

Had he really come to care for her that much already? He was reacting as if it had been his best friend or his brother in danger. Somehow, without him having realized it, Ariel had vaulted herself to the forefront of the group of people who mattered in his life.

That thought scared the hell out of him, too.

"Marco? What's wrong?"

Ariel was waiting for him to say something. Could she tell what he was feeling?

"I'm sorry. I'm just shocked as hell. Can you stay at a neighbor's place until I get there?"

"I think I'm fine here."

"Do you have some kind of information about this guy that you haven't told me? Some reason he'd be out to get you?"

"No, nothing. I mean, I guess he thinks I do, or he's afraid I do, but I really just freaked out when I saw what he was involved in and I got the hell out of there. I didn't stick around to take notes."

"I'll be there in fifteen minutes, okay? Keep your door and windows locked, or go to a neighbor's."

"I'll be here," she said. "Probably packing my bags to leave the country."

LEAVING EUROPE WAS the only thing to do. She would spend the last of her advance on a plane ticket back home. No way would Kostas bother flying all the way to California to find her.

Maybe she'd change her name, go into hiding, assume a new identity....

But she didn't want to leave without having explored this thing with Marco, Ariel realized.

That thought was almost as scary as having a gun pointed at her head.

She grabbed a bag and started packing it. Okay, so she needed to get online and find the next flight for her and the cat to San Francisco before she could actually leave, but nervous energy had her pacing around and frantic.

When she heard a knock at the door, she jumped, then Marco's voice soothed her nerves.

"Ariel, it's me, Marco. Open up."

She let him in and tried not to look as though she was about to burst into tears.

"Are you okay?" he said.

She nodded and went back to her bed to continue packing her bag.

"What are you doing?" he said. "Seriously leaving the country?"

"I'm not going to stick around and tempt fate anymore."

"Just wait a minute." He put himself between her and the bag she was furiously packing. "Maybe I can help you more than you think I can."

"What? You're really Mafioso and you can put out a hit on my ex-boyfriend?"

He didn't smile, and as she looked up at him, she got a little chill down her spine. Not just because he was gorgeous, but because she suddenly had the feeling he wasn't who he had claimed to be.

And after that thought thrilled her, it pissed her off.

"I need to tell you something that you have to keep absolutely secret," Marco said.

Ariel tossed a pair of sandals into her bag. "What? You're going to give me your private e-mail address?"

"I can protect you from this Kostas guy."

"How?"

He stared at her for a while, until she was sure he wasn't going to speak.

"I'm not just a security guard at the embassy," he finally said. "I'm a CIA operative. My name's really Marc."

Part of her wanted to believe him, and part of her was sure he was full of shit.

"Right. And I'm a Russian spy. We're starring in our own bad Cold War spy movie."

"Ariel, I'm serious."

She feigned a Russian accent. "*Zo* am I." A really bad Russian accent.

"I've been a covert operative my entire adult life. I rarely tell anyone my true identity. I'm telling you now, and I need to know you can keep that information private."

She was beginning to get the feeling he wasn't kidding.

"Have you, like, been spying on *me* or something?"

His gaze dropped to the floor for a moment, then back at her, and he smiled sheepishly. "Maybe a little."

"What?" She suddenly felt as if she was standing at the front of her high school auditorium at graduation, stark naked, as had happened in her nightmares.

What could he know about her? The blog? Dear God, not the blog.

"You showed up in a terrorist database because of your relationship with Kostas, that's all."

"But…how did you find me initially?"

"I was watching the embassy security cameras and noticed you watching the place every day— or perhaps watching for Giovanni Lucci, the politician."

Ariel's face burned as she recalled the guy she'd followed like a lunatic. To think that anyone had spotted her doing that… Humiliating.

"Who?" she said, hoping he wasn't who she thought he might be.

"There was a man you seemed to be following. Tall, well-dressed, late thirties?"

Oh.

"Well, were you?"

"What?" She made a lame attempt at stalling.

"Watching him?"

"I didn't realize who he was. I was just kind of… bored, or something."

"You followed him because you were bored?" Marco—Marc clearly wasn't buying it.

"Um, well, yeah… Sort of."

"And what else?"

"I was just attracted to him. He was at the same café as me every morning and I kept trying to work up the nerve to talk to him or something, but I was having kind of a weird…thing."

"A weird thing?"

"I'm normally pretty confident when it comes to men and I usually go after what I want. But after Kostas, I had lost my nerve."

"So you followed Lucci because you were feeling shy?"

"Pretty much. I never did work up the nerve to talk to him, and then you came along and I lost all interest."

A sick feeling invaded her gut as it finally sank in. "Wait a minute—you approached me just to get information, didn't you?"

"Not exactly."

"Then what exactly?"

"I saw you and found you attractive and I was bored, so I decided to investigate."

Ariel slammed her suitcase shut and zipped it.

"Do you always find your dates that way?"

Marc moved between her and the suitcase again. "Don't get all mad and rush out of here. You need to hear me out first."

"You've got thirty seconds."

"I may not have had the purest motives at first, but I figured out over the weekend that your tie to the Greek terrorist was coincidental, and now I'm here because of a true attraction to you and a desire to make sure you don't get hurt by this scumbag."

She glared at him, her heart wanting to believe and her brain screaming that she was a fool if she did.

"Please believe me. That's God's honest truth."

"Why are you telling me this now?"

"Because, like I said, I can protect you. I can put you in a safe house or help you hide out until Kostas is caught."

"I should just go back to the U.S. now and save everyone a lot of trouble."

Marc closed the distance between them and hugged her to him. "I don't want you to go," he said into her hair.

"Why?"

"I like having you around. We have a rare connection, I think."

Ariel's chest tightened. She hated that she could be swayed by such romantic drivel. A rare connection indeed. More likely he wanted to continue to get laid on a regular basis and she knew the moves he liked. There were advantages to sticking with a well-skilled partner for a while rather than going out looking for a new one. She knew the drill, she was the master of it.

"This is too weird." She pushed against his chest until he let go. "You expect me to just be all cool with the fact that you've been spying on me? What else do you know about me from snooping around?"

"Nothing," he said. "You're squeaky clean."

MARC WASN'T EXACTLY PROUD that he was a master liar, especially when it came to lying to his lover. He was pretty sure that violated the rule about non-harm the Buddhists were always talking about. Or maybe it was Right Speech. Or both. He wanted to be able to tell her the truth, and he supposed he could have, but if Ariel knew he had read her blog, there was no way she'd agree to him protecting her.

He had to think of her safety first, and his blemished conscience last.

"Have you snooped around my apartment at all? Checked out my computer? Looked at my phone records?"

"Yes, no and yes."

Her eyebrows shot up. "You have?"

"I'm sorry. It's kind of part of the job, you know."

"Why didn't you check out my computer?"

"You have it password protected and I never had the time to hack in. And after a while I just figured out from everything else that you were clean and there wasn't any reason to keep snooping."

"This is creepy. I've never had anyone admit to spying on me before."

"I'm sorry. It really was just a job to me," he blurted, then realized his mistake too late. "I don't mean—"

"So screwing me was all part of the job." She tried to step around him and grab her bag, but Marc moved to block her again.

"No. It wasn't at all. I have never slept with anyone to get information, I swear."

"Until now." She looked at him as if he were covered in slime, and figuratively, he supposed he was.

"I was attracted to you from the first moment I saw you. That was the reason I flirted, the reason I asked you out and the reason I slept with you."

"And what if I hadn't been flagged as having ties to a terrorist group? Would you have approached me then?"

Marc knew the truth. He wouldn't have, but she would never understand, so he lied. "Yes."

It wasn't completely a lie. If he'd bumped into her in a café or a club or anywhere else, he would have tried to get her attention.

Her posture relaxed a bit, but she cast a doubtful glance at him, then stared at her suitcase.

"So where would you hide me?" she asked after an awkward pause.

"I've given that a little thought. One idea—there's a place near Lake Como. It's secluded and it's stunningly pretty. You can just consider it a vacation."

"I'm going to lose my tutoring job," she said, looking resigned to the idea.

"Maybe not. If you explain—"

"Just explain how my terrorist ex-boyfriend wants to torture and kill me? I'm sure they'll want to keep me around their children."

"Okay, so you just say you have a personal emergency and have to go out of town for a little while."

She was chewing on her lip, but looking more convinced by the second. "So, this lake place. What's the nightly rate? Because my savings have dwindled down to almost nothing and I need at least enough cash to get back to the U.S. if I have to."

"Don't worry about it. We'll be staying for free. It's owned by a friend of mine who only uses it for part of the year."

"Which town is it in?"

"On the outskirts of Bellagio. Lake view, totally secluded from the neighbors. No one will even know we're there unless we want them to."

"After recent events, I have to admit, that sounds blissful."

"We can leave in the morning, and you can stay the night at my place tonight." Marc could hardly believe his luck. "Just let me make a few calls to let people know about Kostas and alert my boss to the fact that I'll be away for a while."

Him. Ariel. Alone in an Italian villa.

Bliss.

Well, aside from all that hiding her from the terrorist stuff.

11

Desperation

Is there a woman alive who hasn't considered lesbianism a sensible alternative to the male gender? I can't be the only one. I guess the only big downside is that, you know, then we wouldn't get to have sex with men.

I love women and all, but let's face it girls, we're missing a key element.

We need the guys.

But that doesn't stop the feeling of desperation that overcomes me every time I think of settling for one guy for the long haul. I mean, really. Just one? I can deal with that for a while, but I guess it's the "for all eternity" thing that gets to me. I mean, isn't that a bit much?

Call me commitment-phobic. That's a well-established fact.

But let's get back to the subject of desperation. I have entered a special state of it recently, in hooking up with X. It's the desperation that comes along with being with a guy I like, and yet knowing it's going to end sooner or later. Probably sooner.

What's your favorite form of sexual desperation?

Comments:
1. Kenya says: I personally am a big fan of being alone and insanely horny, which is the state in which I currently find myself.

2. nuguy says: Where do you live, Kenya? Wanna IM?

3. Eurogirl says: What is this now? The pickup blog?

4. nuguy says: Sorry Eurogirl. Did I break a rule or something?

5. Eurogirl says: No, I'm just feeling angry and bitter than no one is hitting on me. It's supposed to be all about ME, don't you know?!

6. backwoods says: Eurogirl, you're the hottest thing since Tabasco sauce.

7. 2horny says: I'm desperate for a guy who can stay awake for like five seconds after sex.

8. Anonymous says: I'm desperate to find you. And believe me, I know where to look.

9. Willow says: Who is this Anonymous jerk-ass?

Could you please go get a life and stop trolling, you asshole?

10. tanenbaum says: Good to see you back to posting regularly, Eurogirl. We missed you.

11. CKCKCK says: My fav form of desperation is when I have too many women and not enough time for them all.

12. veracruz says: Ah, yes, CK reminds us why we so often wish we could all be lesbians.

13. TiaMaria says: I'm with you girls. We just need to start growing vestigial dicks and we won't need men anymore.

14. tanenbaum says: LOL! Vestigial dicks? Is that anything like superfluous nipples?

15. TiaMaria says: Yes, but dicks are rarely superfluous.

16. Willow says: Mmm, vestigial dick...

MARC HADN'T DRIVEN NORTH of Florence in years, and when the autostrada began snaking into the Dolomites, Italy's portion of the Alps, he couldn't stop craning his neck to admire the scenery.

"I've never been here before," Ariel said as she

gazed out the window at a tall mountain with only a slight trace of white left on top. "It's gorgeous."

"It's been years for me. I'd forgotten how breathtaking it is."

"So this estate we're going to—ever take any other women there?" she asked coyly.

Marc laughed. "No. I did stay there once, visiting my friend who owns it, but I was alone. His family is originally from Italy and they've had the villa for centuries, believe it or not."

"Is the place occupied now?"

"No, they use it for vacations. We'll be completely alone."

Ariel stretched out in her seat and yawned. "I didn't sleep much last night."

"Finding a guy in your apartment aiming a gun at you has that effect."

"Ever happen to you?"

"Once or twice. I've had to infiltrate a few circles where people who shouldn't have guns do."

"That's generally how it works, right? The people who want the guns and have the guns are generally the one we'd least like to have them."

"Pretty much, yeah. But about this Kostas guy— I have a few leads on where he might be staying in Rome, but nothing solid yet."

"You work fast."

"That's my job. There's quite a bit of information on your ex and his network. They have a small cell in Rome, not really active since their concerns are primarily with Greek politics, but they are monitored. It could be he's staying with another member of that network."

Ariel shivered. "Ever since 9/11, I get sick to my stomach at the word *terrorist*. My brother had an internship in the World Trade Center then, and I spent the day crying and frantic, trying to find out if he was still alive."

"I'm sorry."

"I never would have hooked up with Kostas if I'd known what he was involved in."

"We all make the wrong choice in lovers once in a while, but don't worry, we'll catch Kostas before long. Undercover agents are checking out the places he might be staying as we speak. If we find him, we'll hand him over to Greek authorities."

Marc felt his phone vibrate once in his jeans pocket, meaning he'd just received a text message. The only person he could think of who would text him was sitting beside him.

He withdrew his phone from his pocket and looked at the message on the tiny front LCD. It read that he had one new message from Lucia.

"Speaking of wrong choices in lovers, it's a good thing my ex-girlfriend doesn't have a gun," he blurted out, before realizing it probably would have been prudent not to mention how badly he was regarded by some of the women in his past.

Marc imagined Buddha hanging his head in disappointment. Somehow he always managed to confuse the philosophy of "non-harm" with "noncommittal."

"Bad breakup?"

"Not for me. I guess it was bad for her, though, because she's still sending me angry text messages a month later."

He flipped open his phone and read the message, which said simply, "Asshole."

Then he turned the phone so Ariel could see. "Wow. She doesn't waste words, huh?"

"She's an American interpreter who was working at the embassy for a while. Maybe I'm attracted to women with a flair for language," he said. "I mean, you know, since you're an English tutor."

"Yeah, I got it."

Whew. Definitely not because he'd been reading her blog. Absolutely, positively not. For a split second there, he'd again had the urge to let her know he knew about her blog. And he still couldn't say where that impulse had come from, except that it just felt natural to open up to Ariel.

But he wasn't a guy who opened up. In his line of work, that kind of thing could get him killed.

Marc stared ahead at the road and felt his gut twist into a knot. This was all getting too weird. Mixing his work with his personal life had been a mistake, but he couldn't bring himself to turn back now.

He'd never had such intimate access to his lover's thoughts, and he could partly rationalize his behav-

ior as helping him better fulfill her desires. The more
he knew, the better a lover he could be.

Right?

Right.

"Does it bother you that you're still hearing from
your ex?" Ariel asked.

"Sure. I mean, I'd prefer not to hear from her, and
I'd prefer she not still be angry at me."

"What happened?"

"I ended the relationship, and she wasn't ready
for it to end, basically."

"Were things not going well?"

How to answer that one? Marc believed there
was a time and a place to reveal that he was generally considered a jerk by his ex-girlfriends, and right
before a potentially romantic getaway to Bellagio
wasn't it.

"I guess not for me, anyway."

"But she was happy with the relationship, so she
felt blindsided by your wanting out."

"Basically, yeah."

"Been there, done that. It's no fun, I know."

"I should warn you," Marc said, his conscience
getting the best of him. "I'm not known as a guy who
can be counted on to stick around for the long haul."

"Oh?" Ariel sounded almost…amused.

Then he thought of her blog, of all her talk of casual sex and moving on to the next guy, and he
realized…he had finally met his match in the noncommittal department.

"It's partly the nature of my work. I can't get too close, because I'll always be moving on to the next mission."

"And partly just your nature, right?"

"Well…"

"Don't worry, I'm the same. I've had my share of angry exes, trust me."

"Hey, at least I don't have any ex-girlfriends trying to hunt me down and torture me."

"There's one way you can feel good about yourself." He could hear the smile in her voice, and he glanced over at her and smiled back.

"Thanks a bunch. I feel so much better about my playboy ways now."

"Hey, try being a playgirl. Much more frowned upon by society, even today."

"I guess we're a perfect match then, huh? We'll both want out of the relationship sooner rather than later."

"The big question is, who will walk away first?"

"We'd better not go placing any bets," Marc joked, but inside, he was starting to feel anything but lighthearted.

He was starting to feel as though, now that he'd found a woman who was sure to walk away, he wasn't so happy about the idea of parting.

Somewhere along the way, his cover act of playing the eager, interested lover had started being the truth. He really did want to know her now—it wasn't just pretend anymore. His mission had blurred into a real love affair, and he was getting pounded in the gut with why it was bad to mix business with pleasure.

He couldn't find it within himself to pull back, though. And it was absolutely freaking him out.

AFTER A NIGHT in Marc's arms, and with each mile farther they traveled from Rome, Ariel was beginning to feel as if she'd left her problems with Kostas behind for good.

The little Alpine village where they stopped for lunch was a bit out of the way, tucked into a little valley in the Dolomites, but they'd spotted it in the distance and decided to get off the autostrada and check it out on a whim.

The village had been there for centuries, and aside from the crumbling buildings and red stucco rooftops, the most noticeable feature in the town was the towering Catholic church with a tall steeple that echoed the shape of the nearby mountains.

After strolling through the town and buying two sandwiches at the local bakery, along with a bottle of wine from the vintner next door, they headed for an abandoned farmhouse they'd spotted on the way into the village.

Ariel had brought along a blanket from the trunk of the car for them to have a picnic on, and when they reached a shaded spot under an old oak, they spread it out and flopped down.

"Did we wander into a postcard or what?" Marc

said as he lay on the blanket and tucked his hands behind his head. He stared up at the leaves rustling in the breeze, then closed his eyes and yawned.

"You want to sleep for a bit before you eat?"

He opened his eyes, stretched and smiled. "Actually, I had something else in mind."

"Oh?"

"I want *you,* then lunch."

Ariel's body started buzzing instantly. She couldn't get enough of the way he made her instantly aroused, immediately on fire. Without saying another word, she set aside their food and crawled across the blanket to him, draped herself on top of him.

He pulled her close and tickled her lips with his tongue, then took her mouth in a long, exploring kiss. All morning in the car had left her hungry for physical contact with him. She'd watched him drive, studied his hands, his profile, his firm thighs.

She moaned into his mouth, and he pulled back a little to look at her. "I love how you respond to me so eagerly," he said. "It's addictive."

"You're addictive," she whispered, as she trailed kisses along his neck to his ear. "I see now why you were so interested in coming out here to a secluded spot."

"It was making me crazy staring at your legs all morning in the car. I had a raging hard-on half the time."

"I'm surprised I didn't notice."

"You notice it now?"

It was impossible not to. His erection pressed against her, between her legs, making her wetter by the second. She wanted to feel him inside her, but she couldn't resist savoring the desire he stirred in her, the anticipation of what was to come.

Ariel smiled and squirmed against him. "Mmm-hmm," she murmured as she kissed him again. "How could I not?"

"It seems private enough here, right?" He glanced around at their surroundings.

The farmhouse stood with its front door ajar and windows broken—what windows were left—on the other side of a gentle rise in the land. Farther away was a barn, and on the other side of the oak they lay under was a vineyard that had gone to ruin. There wasn't a person in sight.

"Definitely private enough," she said as she sat up and kicked off her sandals, then reached under her skirt and tugged off her panties.

He arched an eyebrow. "You don't waste any time."

She smiled as she started unfastening his pants. "We should probably leave our clothes on, just in case we get interrupted, don't you think?"

The sight of his bare cock made her smile, as he probably hadn't worn any boxers today in anticipation of an occasion such as this.

"Sure," he said, but then she had her hand on his cock, and he seemed to lose all interest in further conversation.

He closed his eyes and sighed as she began to stroke him, lightly at first. He leaked a slippery fluid that she rubbed on the head of his dick and used to lubricate her hand, too, as she moved it along his shaft. She leaned down and kissed the spot where the fluid came out, and then she flicked her tongue out and around him as he gasped and squirmed at the sensations.

Ariel wanted to feel as if he was just another sexual conquest, as if he was just another guy for her blog. But somehow, finding her perfect lover was having consequences she hadn't begun to anticipate. Her feelings weren't as removed from the experience as they usually were, and she wasn't so easygoing about it all.

She barely recognized herself lately.

Maybe it was the whole thing with Kostas that had her thinking and feeling differently.

She took Marc into her mouth and sucked his shaft, in and out in a steady rhythm, savoring him as she teased at his balls with her fingertips.

Sure, she was still the same sex-obsessed Ariel in some ways, but ever since finding out her boyfriend was a terrorist, feelings had been welling that she'd never experienced before. Not only did it make her think of the fear she'd felt on September 11 and the looming question in her mind of what really mattered in life when she thought she'd lost the only person she loved, but it made her ask herself that question in a much more immediate way.

What really did matter to her? What was the point of her life? Did she really want to live just for the sake of hedonistic pleasures? Didn't she have any greater purpose?

And why was she asking herself such weighty questions in the middle of a blow job?

She withdrew a bit and stroked his cock by hand again, trying to force her thoughts back to the present moment.

"Is something wrong?" Marc asked. "You seem distracted."

"I'm sorry. I was just thinking of this whole mess, my having to go into hiding—all that."

"It's stressful, I know, but you don't need to worry. We'll find the guy, and you'll be free to live your life like a normal person again."

He took her hand away from his cock and pulled her up until she was lying beside him. She rested her head on his chest and sighed.

"I'm sorry," Ariel said. "I don't want to ruin a perfectly great moment with my wayward thoughts."

"It's okay. I'm glad you told me. It's easy for me to forget that normal people aren't used to being in serious danger. I've lived with the everyday threat of harm for so long it's second nature to me."

"It doesn't bother you at all?"

"No. I just learned to look at it as a part of life that I've had to acknowledge more than most people are forced to. I'm just as likely to be killed in a car accident or by cancer or some other bad luck as I am to be killed on the job."

"Hey, there's a cheery thought."

"Yeah, sorry, I'm full of those. It's how I put the whole danger thing in perspective."

Ariel's body was still buzzing with desire, even if her brain had refused to cooperate. She needed to get their little afternoon tryst back on track before it was too late. She needed less talk and more action.

Besides, she was seriously not liking the thought of Marc constantly in danger. And she didn't want to sit around and consider why the idea left her feeling so paralyzed with fear.

She leaned on her elbow so she could look him in the eye. "I promise to put the morbid thoughts out of my head if you promise to shut up and do me now."

He smiled slowly. "You're trying to distract me with sex, aren't you?"

"No," she said and gave his chest a little shove.

"You are. Why?"

Ariel rolled her eyes. "In my experience, there's not a man alive who isn't permanently distracted by sex. You can't blame me for that."

He rolled over and forced her onto the blanket beneath him. His hard body pressed her back into the ground, and when his mouth was only a few inches from hers, he said, "I don't know what's really bothering you, but I know that no amount of sexual enticement is going to distract me from caring what it is."

"I'm sorry. I didn't mean to trivialize your concern. You've been nothing but sweet and helpful to me from the start."

"You're going to have to learn sooner or later that my interest is genuine."

"I do know that."

"If you really knew it, you'd stop trying to keep our relationship on a purely sexual level."

Marc's gaze held hers in challenge, as if he was daring her to open up emotionally. And it was a dare she both did and didn't want to take.

"That's what you think I'm trying to do?"

"I know you are."

She considered protesting, but he'd nailed her, and there was no sense in denying it now. "It's an old habit," she said. "Nothing against you personally."

"Gee, thanks. That makes me feel all better."

"What do you want me to say?" She felt a tightness forming in her throat, threatening to cut off all her lame protests and reveal her as the coward she really was.

"I want you to say you won't keep retreating from me. At least give feeling something besides sexual pleasure with me a chance. Can you do that?"

"Of course I can. I will. I promise."

But did she mean it? Could she really give him a chance?

Ariel knew herself pretty well when it came to

men, but what she didn't know was how she behaved when it came to Marc. That's what scared her most. He was nothing like the other men she'd known. And with him, all bets about her ability to remain sane and in control were off.

Despite his declaration that he wasn't in it for the long haul, she was beginning to suspect he represented everything she couldn't handle—love, commitment and excruciating pain.

The idea gave her an even bigger scare than the thought of addiction. A sexual addiction could be kicked with a plane ticket to a different country, or perhaps a twelve-step program, but what was the cure for a doomed emotional entanglement?

There wasn't one. There was just the frightening sensation of knowing she was careening out of control toward a crash, and there would be pain. Lots of it.

MARC SLID HIS HANDS up Ariel's bare thigh and under her dress, and in a moment his dick was pressed against her wet pussy and he was on the verge of entering her. Then he recalled the need for a damn condom and he paused long enough to find one in his pocket and put it on.

He lay on top of her, with the skirt of her dress pushed up to her waist, and he eased himself inside her slowly. He'd never in his life find anything or anyone who felt better than Ariel. If this was it, the pinnacle of his sex life, he would savor it for all he was worth and be glad of the relationship, whether it lasted much longer or not.

He watched pleasure soften her features, desire clouding her warm brown gaze, and his dick grew even harder at her beauty. She was naturally beautiful not because of her even features and obvious sex appeal, but because of something that radiated from within her. She was confident and at ease with herself, and it showed in the way she moved, the way she interacted with the world.

A lump formed in Marc's throat as he gazed into her eyes, and he started moving inside her, wanting more than anything to make her relax enough to just accept whatever came their way for as long as they could have it.

So what if they didn't last forever. Right now was pretty damn great and wasn't that the best any relationship could hope for?

Her eyes fluttered shut, and he covered her mouth in a long deep kiss. She wrapped her legs around his hips, opening herself wider to him, and his cock throbbed with restrained pleasure. He just wanted to go as deep as possible inside her, to feel her warmth all over him, to be surrounded by her perfect flesh and her intoxicating scent.

It scared him a little, how badly he wanted her.

So it wasn't as though he didn't understand her fear. He did. But he also knew from experience that fear wasn't something to cower away from.

Buddhist teachings talked about embracing one's

fear, acknowledging it and learning to understand it for what it is. That, if nothing else, helped him keep it all in perspective.

"Just let me in," he whispered. "Let me really know you."

"I will," she murmured against his lips. "I will."

He thrust into her again and again, wanting to be in her both literally and figuratively. Wanting his physical act to somehow express his emotional desire. He savored her heat and her warmth as the midday air added a delicious extra dimension to their pleasure.

Nothing like the outdoors to make good sex feel even better. Marc could feel the tension of climax building inside him already, and he wanted to delay it. He thrust into her a few times more, gradually slowing, then eased out of her and inched his way down her body.

Stopping at her breasts, he pushed aside her dress and was thrilled to find her, as he'd suspected, without a bra. He teased her nipples with his tongue, tasting her sweet warm flesh, wanting to drink her in all day. Forget wine. Ariel was the nectar of the gods as far as he was concerned.

When she was squirming and whimpering, her fingers twined in his hair, he moved lower, trailing kisses down her rib cage, across her belly, until his mouth was between her legs where he wanted to be. He plunged his tongue into her wet folds and lapped at her gently, getting drunker by the second at the taste of Ariel.

She was the greatest delicacy he'd ever tasted, and he could never get enough.

He moaned against her warm flesh, rubbed his tongue against her clit and held her hips as she squirmed. She arched up to meet his mouth, giving in to the intense sensations, letting his tongue go where it pleased.

He plunged his fingers into her slippery depths and sucked until she was gasping and whimpering, her body tensed at the edge of release. He loved controlling her this way, loved that he had the power to turn her into a woman consumed by desire.

And then, with a few flicks of his tongue, he sent her over the edge.

Ariel cried out with the strength of her orgasm, gasping, uttering little sounds of pleasure as the waves of her release washed over her. A light breeze had kicked up, and it swept over the hillside to cool them, at the same time rustling the leaves of the oak tree and sprinkling dappled light across Ariel.

He gazed up at her from between her legs, amazed at how beautiful she was, amazed at how she endlessly captured his imagination.

He was in deep, deep danger. He knew it, and he embraced it. There was no other way to deal with fear. There was no other way to live.

He inhaled Ariel's musky sweet scent one more time before moving up and positioning himself between her legs again. While she was still limp from her release, still catching her breath, he sank his cock into her and began thrusting again.

Whatever else they were to each other, and whatever dangers Ariel posed to his sanity and his heart, he knew that right here, right now, was exactly where they were supposed to be. And he had every intention of enjoying the moment for all it was worth.

He held her thigh with one hand and braced himself on his other elbow as he came closer and closer to his own release, his body tense with pleasure, his gaze locked on Ariel's face. He wanted her to see exactly how she affected him, and he wanted to come while staring into her eyes.

The orgasm sneaked up on him unexpectedly, racking his body as he spilled into her, as shock waves of pleasure rendered him limp and spent on top of her. He kissed her again, this time more slowly—a thank-you kiss.

"Wow," he whispered against her lips. "That was amazing."

"There's something about open-air sex, an added layer of stimulation from the fresh air and the sounds of nature."

"Whatever it was, it gave me the best orgasm I've had in a long time."

She smiled. "Me, too."

They curled up against each other for a short while, resting, until Ariel wriggled under him again.

"Hungry?" Marc asked.

"We should probably eat and get going soon, right? I don't think we want to get into Bellagio after dark and have to find our way around then."

"Yeah. I'm not that familiar with the place." He sat up and watched her as she stood. Seeing her gorgeous body disappear as her dress fell down over her hips again was enough to drive him crazy.

Marc grabbed her leg and held her so she couldn't move away. "I don't think I'm finished with you."

"What?" Ariel peered down at him, looking confused.

He stood on his knees and backed her up to the trunk of the tree, then lifted her skirt. "I think I'd rather have you for lunch than that sad little sandwich."

She smiled. "You just had me for lunch, in case you've already forgotten."

"I want seconds."

She leaned back against the tree and parted her thighs a bit to grant him easier access. "You won't hear me arguing."

Marc kissed the curls at the apex of her thighs, then flicked his tongue between her legs, along her clit. She closed her eyes and gasped, reaching up to hold on to a branch to steady herself.

He couldn't get enough of the scent and taste of her, as he began sucking at her, drinking her in. As her breath quickened and her body tensed, he worked his tongue against her in a steady rhythm, pausing only to nibble. She truly was a delicacy.

Where did he go after this? What other woman

could compare after he'd had someone so responsive, so…everything he'd ever desired?

He didn't want to know.

He just wanted to keep going, keep exploring how deep they could get, how close, how intimate.

How *intimate?*

It wasn't a state he'd ever really tried to achieve, but somehow, with Ariel, it seemed like the ultimate goal—true, deep intimacy.

He was beginning to sound like a changed man. Really great sex could do that to a guy, Marc supposed.

She was still wet from her last come, but now she was getting even wetter the closer she came to orgasm. He slid one hand up her thigh and dipped his fingers into her as he continued massaging her with his tongue. Soon he felt her quaking with her second release.

Holding her to him, he experienced the waves of her climax washing over her. The sounds of her gasping aroused him anew, but he didn't want to make her wait for lunch any longer, so he ignored his erection and stood up to kiss her.

Ariel's eyes were half-lidded, clouded with desire, and she smiled at him lazily. "You're too kind."

"No, you're too kind to let me do that again. I think I have a craving for you."

"I'll be happy to oblige you anytime." She kissed him one more time, then turned to get their lunch.

Marc watched as she took out the sandwiches

and wine, and he found the bottle opener and opened it for them. They drank straight from the bottle and ate their sandwiches in silence, listening to the sounds of the countryside.

He'd never felt this content before. He'd never felt so right, so at home, with a woman before. And now that he did, it was a feeling he didn't want to let go of.

He knew he'd have to eventually, but until then, he had to find a way to convince Ariel that intimacy wasn't such a bad thing. Even with a serial dater, it could be a worthwhile pursuit while it lasted.

12

One Woman's Trash Is Another Woman's Pleasure

Is it true that when it comes to sex, one woman's trash is another woman's treasure? Or, should I say, pleasure?

If you've ever been with someone who's had previous lovers, you know that they've probably been trashed by someone else at one point or another. I, for one, have been dumpee and dumper both, more times than I would like to count.

I was with X the other day when he heard from an ex-girlfriend, who was sending him a nasty text message. Nasty, as in, she thinks he's a bastard and was just writing to let him know. And it occurred to me that a lot of women might take that as a big warning sign.

But I don't think you can really tell everything from anyone's success or lack thereof in previous relationships. Yet I do believe our track records say a lot about us. We just might not be able to properly interpret their meaning, or want to hear what they're saying when we do.

ARIEL REREAD her blog entry and clicked the Save to Drafts button instead of posting it now. She wasn't sure she was making any sense, and she figured she probably needed to think about the subject for a bit before posting. Also Marc was about to come back in the house and she didn't want to get busted.

She closed her computer and tucked it away in its bag, safe from prying eyes, then picked up the cell phone to call her landlord back in Rome, who was cat-sitting Angelina.

AFTER THREE IDYLLIC DAYS at the estate outside of Bellagio, Marc was frustrated by the lack of progress his colleagues had reported in tracking down Kostas, but he could hardly call himself frustrated in bed. Ariel was tireless and endlessly creative. And he was having the time of his life.

It was easy to forget he was supposed to be a diligent CIA operative when he had a beautiful sex-obsessed woman distracting him constantly.

"Are you into bondage? A little blindfolding maybe?" A wicked smile crept across Ariel's face as she opened the closet and withdrew a handful of silk scarves.

Marc hated having to be a spoilsport. "Eh, I don't think it's really my thing."

"Oh, come on! Who doesn't like to lose control every once in a while?"

"Me?" Marc pushed himself up on the bed and leaned against the headboard.

Ariel sat down on the edge of the bed beside him and traced her fingers across his abdomen.

"Is this because of your spy training or something? You think I'm going to tie you up with my faux Fendi scarves and torture you for information?"

He tried not to grin. "Maybe."

"If I torture you, it will be in the best kind of way."

"Oh?"

"I might tease you relentlessly with sexual pleasure, make you hold off for hours, bring you to the brink over and over again and then pull back until I've turned you into a quivering mass of need. That kind of thing."

"Where do I sign up?" he said sarcastically.

She snapped a scarf between her hands. "Do I have to get rough with you to get my way?"

"I'm just not into the whole losing control thing. I'm sorry."

The sound of cars honking drifted up the hill into the open window for a few moments—a sharp contrast to the languid, sensual mood in the bedroom of the villa. Ariel had lit candles, and a fan across the room was set on low, stirring the warm air. A small stereo played a Barry White CD.

She wore only a black lace bra and panties, and probably every other heterosexual guy on earth would have agreed to let her tie him up and whip him if she wanted to. But Marc had a wall of resistance to losing control that he knew she probably couldn't break down—and even if she could, he was pretty damn sure he wouldn't enjoy himself.

She was watching him carefully. "Do you trust me?"

Trust. It wasn't something he ever took lightly. "I'm still getting to know you."

"Which means no, you don't."

"I'm sorry, it's just part of my job, I guess. Trust no one and suspect everyone. I have to live my life that way."

She was trying not to look hurt, but he could tell she was anyway. "Doesn't that suck?"

"Yeah, pretty much."

"Have you ever completely trusted someone?"

Marc considered the question, and there wasn't any answer that was going to make him sound good. He'd been a natural as a clandestine operative, because even as a kid he'd learned that trust wasn't a thing to bestow lightly...or ever.

"Not completely, no."

She stared at him as if he'd just revealed a cancer diagnosis. "Wow," she said. "I'm sorry."

"I guess you see now why me and long-term relationships don't get along."

"Who do you turn to when you need a friend to lean on, or you just need to get something off your chest?"

"I don't. It's just part of my work—I learn to keep secrets and rely only on myself."

"But don't you have to work with other people sometimes?"

"Sure, with the knowledge that they might betray me at any time."

"Didn't you trust anyone as a child, even?"

"Maybe before I knew any better."

"Were you raised by wolves or something?"

Marc smiled ironically. "Wolves would probably have been more nurturing."

She raised her eyebrows, but said nothing, waiting for him to continue.

"I mentioned my dad was in the foreign service, but I didn't say that my mom left when my brother and I were young."

"How young?"

"I was one and David was three."

Ariel winced. "Ouch. I'm sorry."

"Hey, we all need something to rebel against, right?"

"You really believe that?"

He shrugged. "Sure."

"Have you been in contact with your mom since she left?"

Marc shook his head. "She was manic-depressive and, according to my dad, she ended up living in Paris with some performance artist until she committed suicide by overdosing."

"Oh, God, I'm so sorry. Did your dad ever remarry?"

"Sure, he married the Ice Queen. Neither one of them could handle having two little boys running around disrupting their lives, so…"

"So that's why you were shipped off to boarding school."

"Basically, yeah. The official party line was that we were getting a world-class education."

"Were you close to your dad at all?"

"As close as I could be seeing him only during summers and holiday vacations."

"How about now?"

"He lives in Monterey with the Ice Queen. He plays golf and smokes cigars and plots how to protect his money from being taxed."

"Do you talk?"

"Occasionally, but he's really pretty old-school about emotional issues. He figures a good stiff drink is the solution to most problems, and if I ever tried to have a real heart-to-heart conversation with him, he'd probably think I was gay."

"I can see why being raised by wolves doesn't sound so bad to you."

Marc glanced down at the scarves in her hand and felt pang of guilt that he'd killed the mood. At least now she'd understand why he was so screwed up. Better that she find out now rather than later.

"I should come with a warning label, huh? Beware—Emotionally Damaged."

She smiled sadly. "I think if we were being honest, we'd probably all have to wear some kind of label like that."

"You seem pretty well-adjusted."

"Right. Given my family life, I guess I've survived okay."

"But you're still damaged?"

"Sure. We all are."

"You never talk about your family, either."

She sighed and stretched out beside him on the bed. "Probably for the same reasons you don't."

"You should have been raised by wolves, too?"

"I actually *was*." Ariel laughed, but there wasn't any humor in it. "My parents weren't really equipped to be responsible adults. They were both addicts always looking for the next fix."

"Is that why your brother became an addict?"

"Pretty much. You grow up watching your parents get high and you can't help seeing it as a possible solution when your life gets rough."

"How about you?"

"Other than alcohol and a brief flirtation with Mary Jane as a teenager, I've got a spotless history. I learned to stay away from the hard stuff by seeing what it did to my parents."

"Your brother wasn't so lucky."

"He fell in with the wrong crowd. I tried to protect him, but I could only do so much, especially when I was trying to get my own life in order."

Marc snaked his arm around her and pulled her close. She had a streak of altruism in her that he found irresistible. It was impossible not to see how clearly she loved her brother.

He placed a soft kiss on her forehead and inhaled

her sweet scent. She smelled like home. She felt like home. She had a dangerous, addictive effect on his psyche that scared the hell out of him.

"He's lucky to have you as a sister."

"Try and tell him that since I ran off to Europe and never came back."

"Does he resent your leaving?"

"Oh, yeah. I'm his whole family, and he thinks I've abandoned him."

"You don't go home for holidays or anything?"

She shook her head. "He's come here a few times, but I haven't gone back. I get sick to my stomach just thinking about it."

"So why are you leaving Italy in September?"

Ariel was silent for a few moments. "It's a weird thing. I'm going back for my brother's wedding, but I've been feeling lately like my time in Europe is coming to a permanent end."

"Do you ever miss California?"

"Sure, there are lots of things I miss. I think it's just the emotional stuff that I'm afraid of going back and facing."

"But you're going to do it anyway. That takes some courage."

"It's probably nothing so noble as that. I kind of always had it in my head that I'd travel around Europe for five years and then I'd go home."

"Why five years?"

"It just sounded like a good idea at the time, I guess."

She draped her leg over his, and his dick stirred in his boxers. His gaze dropped to the hint of brown hair showing through her panties, and he went hard all the way. Damn good timing he had, getting all horny in the middle of their heart-to-heart talk. Yet another reason he made a lousy long-term partner.

She noticed the tent that had formed in his boxers and smiled. Her hand slid down his belly, stopping at the elastic waistband.

"I'm sorry. I didn't mean to distract you from our talk."

"Talk is cheap, right?" she whispered, and before he could stop her, she'd snaked her way down and was brushing her lips against the head of his cock through the thin cotton underwear.

Marc closed his eyes and sighed. Whatever else she was, Ariel was the most exciting woman he'd ever had the pleasure of knowing. If ever there was a substance he could become addicted to, she was it. She was the biggest danger he'd ever faced, and he couldn't decide if he should let himself sink into the addiction, or turn and run like hell.

ARIEL TOOK HIM INTO her mouth and moaned softly at the delicious hard length of him. She couldn't get enough of Marc's dick. She couldn't get enough of him, period.

And the whole heart-to-heart talk thing—she hadn't really meant for it to happen. But something about him made her want to open up and share all the ugly truths that she generally went around shielding from the world. She wanted him to know her, to really know her as no one else did.

Which was incredibly stupid.

She couldn't kid herself about what kind of relationship this was. It was the kind of relationship she always had. The sexual kind. The emotional arm's-length kind. The let's-don't-have-any-expectations kind.

Marc, more than any of her recent lovers, needed to be kept at a distance. His whole fear of being tied up was a perfect example. Talk about trust issues.

And talk about Mommy issues.

The guy was a walking emotional time bomb. Not a guy to be counted on for more than great sex.

She ran the tip of her tongue up and down the length of him, then pulled off his boxers and took his balls into her mouth as she stroked his shaft. He squirmed and gasped at the sensations, while she closed her eyes and tried to forget what they'd talked about.

She didn't want to start caring for him, didn't want to open herself up to some big emotional free-fall, but she could feel herself slipping off the safe ledge she'd created. And soon she'd be facing the hard ground below. Hurtling at full speed toward it, if she wasn't careful.

Usually, there was nothing like a blow job to get her focused on the here and now. She loved the in-timacy and power of it, loved bestowing such pleasure on another person, loved the whole sensual experience. But right now, their conversation kept echoing in her head.

She took him into her mouth again and began a slow, steady rhythm with her lips and tongue. Marc's breath grew ragged and shallow, while his hand cupped the back of her head.

The physical relationship should have been enough. She was happy with the emotional buffer she'd created around her life, a protective guard against more hurt.

But something about him beckoned to her.

He made her wonder if she was walking through life sedated, if she was missing out on great pleasure in all her efforts to avoid any more pain.

With him, the physical relationship was feeling as if it wasn't enough. As if it needed to be connected to something deeper.

Goddamn it.

She could feel him getting close to orgasm, and she slowed, then pulled away, fully intending to tease him just as she'd promised. Even if he didn't go for the obvious loss of control through bondage, she still knew how to take control of a man's body.

But her mind kept circling around the idea of trust. Who deserved it. Who didn't. Did she deserve to be trusted? She'd never betrayed a man, never cheated, never lied…unless one counted the anonymous sex blog thing as a betrayal.

And maybe it was. She never asked anyone's consent before discussing their sexual activities. She simply used the anonymity as her justification. But if any of her lovers ever found out about the blog, she doubted they'd be thrilled. Especially when they read all her descriptions of encounters with other men.

Kostas had nearly discovered her blog by walking into the room while she was composing an entry. He'd attempted to read over her shoulder, and she'd just barely kept her activity hidden. At least she was pretty sure she had, until those comments from Anonymous began to appear.

At the time, she'd said she'd simply been writing and that she didn't like anyone reading her rough drafts. True. She'd admitted to a desire to be published someday—also true. No need to mention that her blog gave her an instant forum for the world to read. And she'd said she simply wrote about her travels. Definitely not true.

All in all, she'd made it sound quite innocent, which, she supposed, it wasn't.

So maybe Marc was right not to trust her.

But she still didn't like it.

She wanted him to think more of her, to think she was different from other women. Special somehow.

Stupid thing to want.

Stupid, stupid, stupid.

"What's wrong?" Marc said, and Ariel felt a flush of embarrassment that she'd committed one of the ultimate blow job faux pas.

She'd gotten distracted during sex again, damn it.

If physical pleasure was a sort of wall she'd built to protect herself from further intimacy, Marc was breaking it down. Sex wasn't working as her barrier now.

He pulled her up to face him.

"Nothing," she said. "Really."

"It's something we were talking about, isn't it?"

Ariel sighed and pushed her hair out of her face, stared out the window at the waning evening light. The candles were all that illuminated the room now.

She didn't know what to say. She both loved and hated that he was so perceptive about her feelings and changes of mood. Perhaps that was one of the many disadvantages of dating a spy—they were trained to read people.

Ariel didn't like being read. She had too many parts of herself she wanted to keep private.

"It's nothing," she said halfheartedly, angry at herself for not being able to put on a better act.

"I can tell." His voice dripped sarcasm.

Ariel went silent, still staring out the window. The lush greenery outside, along with the glistening blue lake down below, should have been a soothing sight, but in the fading light, it all just looked bleak and lonely to her.

"If I said something that's bothering you, I'm sorry," he said.

"You don't trust me," she blurted and immediately regretted it. It had come out sounding like a pouty accusation.

"I don't trust anyone, so don't take it personally."

"Isn't all of this personal, though? Don't we have to have some trust to be lovers?"

"If this is about tying me up—"

"No, it's about your being able to repeatedly sleep with someone you don't trust. How do you do that?"

"Same way most people can have a one-night stand, I guess."

"So this is just an extended one-night stand?" She wished like hell she could shut herself up.

She was sounding dangerously close to being a person who gave a damn.

He sighed, looking resigned. "I thought that's what you wanted it to be. You've been just as guilty of holding me at arm's length as anyone."

True. But…

But what? What the hell was wrong with her?

"I'm sorry. I'm sounding like a spoiled child. I guess I've just never had anyone be so frank about not trusting me, and it struck me is all."

"It's me, not you." Marc reached out and caressed her cheek, but she pulled back.

"Maybe I'm really not trustworthy, though. This is the first time the idea has ever occurred to me."

"You want honesty?"

She scowled at him. "No, please, lie to me."

"You do come across as a woman with some secrets. I'm not sure what they are, but I know they're there."

"Doesn't everyone have secrets?"

"Sure, but not everyone lives their life by them. Yours seem to dominate you somehow."

"Thanks for the analysis, Dr. Phil. Are you going to give me my tough-love solution now?"

Ariel started grabbing her clothes from the floor and getting dressed.

He grasped her arm and tried to turn her to face him, but she pulled away.

"Since you can read my mind, tell me what I'm thinking now, asshole." She was immediately ashamed at her inability to control her temper.

"I'll go," he said.

And as she watched him dress, she wondered if she'd ever find a guy for whom she'd want to truly lay herself bare. A guy who could be the keeper of her secrets, the one who knew her inside and out.

Some treacherous, awful voice in her head piped up and said that Marc was that guy.

13

He's Got It Going On

Is there any feeling more blissful than finding a lover you know you're in the groove with? I can count on one hand the number of times I've clicked with a guy right away, without any special effort or toys to make it all work, so to speak.

Can I get an "amen" for the guys who know how to work what they've got?

I have a thing for selfless lovers. I like a guy to be so caught up in giving pleasure that he's at least as interested in giving it as he is in receiving it. I like to think of these guys as the Mahatma Gandhi of the bedroom. Performing noble oral service to aid humanity.

I mean, let's face it, wouldn't the world be a better place if everyone were getting really good oral?

Of course, that means we all have to be committed to giving it, too. So that's my challenge to all you readers out there. Make going down your mission in life. Make it your raison d'être. Learn every technique, every nuance of giving pleasure with your mouth, and practice, practice, practice.

You'll be doing the world a great service.

Comments:
1. DonJuan says: Amen, sista.

2. dogman says: I volunteer to be the practice guy for any women who need a partner for their learning process.

3. KendraK says: dream on, dogman

4. Max M says: I agree, Eurogirl. Oral sex is probably the key to world peace.

5. Eurogirl says: Hey, if I were running the world, oral would be a key part of all diplomatic talks.

6. juju says: I'm so envious. Could you please stop bragging about all the good sex you're getting?

7. Eurogirl says: Sorry, I'm being a bit obnoxious, huh?

8. Willow says: Gandhi would be proud of you, Eurogirl.

9. Anonymous says: I haven't forgotten about you, Ariel. You can't hide from me.

10. juju says: Hey, Anonymous, stop being an asshole and get lost.

ARIEL CHOKED on her San Pellegrino at the sight of comment # 9. She coughed and sputtered until she cleared her windpipe of the mineral water, and then hurriedly deleted the comment, her heart racing at the fact that even her first name had appeared on her blog for a few hours, for the whole world to see.

What if she had to shut down her blog? The anonymous poster could clearly do whatever the hell he wanted. She'd tried to ignore his posts before now, but mentioning her by name was just too much. If he knew her identity, he could post anything he wanted about her. He could ruin her, or worse.

She didn't know what he knew. But she was sure he knew too much. And she was pretty damn sure it was Kostas doing the posting.

She forced herself to take deep breaths, in and out slowly, until her heart was no longer racing. Then she deleted the next post, as well, since it referred to the offending comment. Then she e-mailed juju and explained why her comment had been erased.

The anonymous poster hadn't left an e-mail address when he'd logged in. She could make doing so a requirement to post in her blog, but anonymous e-mail accounts were so easy to create, it was pointless. That extra layer of security would only serve to annoy and inconvenience her loyal readers.

"What's the matter? You look like you're about

to smash your computer," Marc said, looming in the doorway next to her.

He caught her miserable expression. "What's wrong?"

"You're out of beer, and I want one."

"No we're not. I just came back from the store. There's a new six-pack chilling in the fridge as we speak."

"Oh," she said too stiffly. "Good."

"Is that really what's wrong?"

She sighed. Did she dare tell him the truth? The whole truth? Her stomach lurched at the thought, but she needed to get this crap off her chest, too.

She thought of having Marc read everything she'd written about him, and she felt like throwing up.

But what other choice did she have? He was a CIA operative trying to hide her from a terrorist, and if she didn't give him all the information she had, how could he help her?

"I have this, um, blog," she said. "Where I talk to my friends online and stuff, and Kostas has been posting there, I think, threatening me."

Marc's gaze was inscrutable. "Do you have a post on it from him now?"

"Yeah, well, I did."

"You didn't delete it, did you?"

She winced. "Yeah, I did. I freaked out."

"Damn it! We could try to trace where he's posting from if you'd left the comment there."

"I'm sorry. I wasn't thinking—"

"Next time, just come get me, okay? I'll deal with it."

"I should probably take my blog off-line for a while, huh?" she said, but she hated the idea.

She'd never once shut it down since she began three years ago, and she didn't want to lose the readers she had.

"No, you shouldn't. It's a link to this guy. He'll post again, and it's a way we can try to find him."

"But what if he posts my last name, too, next time? What if he—"

"I can have someone set up a monitoring system for the Web site, so that every time someone creates a new post, we'll be notified on your cell phone, and we can hide any inappropriate comments right away."

Ariel winced at the idea. At any given time, anyone and everyone in the world could be looking at her blog. She had an average of five thousand visitors to the site a day. Five thousand potential invaders of her privacy, if they knew her real name.

"I don't know," she said. "The stuff I write on it is kind of private, and really, I'm not sure I'd want you reading it, either."

He frowned. "Why not?"

She shrugged, trying to act casual. "It's just girl talk kind of stuff. I generally don't like my boyfriends reading it."

Marc raised an eyebrow, then came to her side and leaned over to read what was on the computer screen. There for him and all the world to see was her rambling about oral sex and its potential effect on world peace.

Ariel hurriedly closed the window to hide the post.

"I don't want you reading any good stuff I wrote about you and have it go to your head," she said as an excuse.

"Believe me, babe. It can't help but go to my head, if you know what I mean."

She laughed, but it came out sounding a little forced.

Ariel would never get used to the idea of one of her lovers actually knowing about and reading what she was posting. Knowing Kostas had probably read everything was bad enough. It had made her far more inhibited about what she wrote.

She couldn't deal with Marc reading the blog, too.

"If it freaks you out too much, I won't read your blog, okay?"

"Thank you," she said. "I'm sorry to be such a spaz about it, and I guess if we don't catch Kostas soon, I'll have to let you read it anyway."

He took her hand and pulled her up to a standing position, then dipped his head and kissed her long and deep.

"It turns me on to know you're talking to your friends about me."

She smiled a little. "Yeah?"

"Oh, yeah."

She could feel his erection pressing against her now.

"Well, then that's an unexpected benefit."

He slid his hands up under her top and found her bra clasp, then undid it. A moment later, his hands were caressing her breasts, tugging at her nipples, sending shock waves of pleasure from there downward.

"I think I still need to do lots of impressive stuff so you'll tell them more good things about me."

"Mmm," she moaned. "I think you've got the right idea."

"Oh, I do, trust me."

Marc pushed her top up and sat down in the desk chair, then pulled her between his legs and took her left breast into his mouth. Ariel craved him so much, and in so many ways, it was always a relief to feel him giving her pleasure—a relief from the constant, sweet aching.

She'd never had a lover she desired so constantly, a lover she wanted so completely and felt herself bonding to so strongly.

It was almost as if she was falling in love.

Love. The idea jolted her out of her blissful state of arousal and back into harsh reality. The true nature of their relationship was impermanent, transient, fleeting. Deluding herself was the last trap she needed to fall into now.

She had to get control of herself and remember why they were really here. Strictly for the sex.

She closed her eyes again and forced the negative thoughts away, focusing instead on the delicious pleasure Marc had wrought on her breasts. He had taken each nipple into his mouth in turn, sucking and coaxing her into an almost unbearable state of arousal.

At the same time, one of his hands had slipped beneath her skirt and was traveling up her thigh. His fingertips brushed against her panties, quickly finding her clit through the fabric and stroking her there in an achingly slow silky rhythm.

She gasped at the pleasure, and her mind instantly cleared of whatever worrisome thoughts had been plaguing her moments ago.

He tugged her panties down, and they fell to her ankles. Then he slipped his fingers inside her wet opening and stroked her from the inside, finding her G-spot.

Ariel's breath grew shallow, and she murmured, "Don't stop."

Not that he ever did. He always knew when to keep going, when to pull back, when to tease and when to go for the finish line. He understood the rhythms of her body better than anyone ever had.

She tangled her fingers in his hair and pressed his mouth harder against her breast. He grazed her nipple with his teeth, mingling the pleasure with a deliciously gentle pain.

Then he pushed her back and dropped out of the chair to his knees, tugged off her skirt and buried his tongue in her. Ariel lifted her leg and propped it on the chair to accommodate him better, and his tongue against her clit nearly caused her to come immediately.

He knew her body too well. It was scary how hard it would be to find an adequate lover after having been with Marc.

Damn scary.

Ariel rocked her hips gently against his mouth, and he slid his fingers inside her again as he licked her. She was dripping wet, and her muscles were coiling tighter and tighter, threatening to bring her to orgasm at any moment.

Then, reading her body like a book, he pulled back ever so slightly, slowing down her excitement to make it last.

It was true. When Marc was gone from her life, as he inevitably would be, she'd have a hell of a time finding a replacement.

MARC WAS ADDICTED to the taste of her. If he could have spent the entire day between Ariel's legs, he would have. But she was too selfless a lover to ever let that happen. He'd have to convince her that the truly selfless act was not bringing him pleasure—but letting him bring her release, over and over again.

She wasn't so far off with that blog entry of hers. All the action was really in loving to give satisfaction. That's where things got interesting. Anyone could lie around and let someone service them, but it took true talent to learn another person's body.

And Ariel's was such a pleasure to learn.

He sucked at her and rubbed his tongue against her, savoring her musky scent, her delicious wet folds. He loved feeling her come against his mouth, but just as much, he loved the slow buildup. She was such a responsive lover, it was actually hard to create a slow buildup with Ariel, but he had learned which buttons to push and when, to drag out the delicious experience as long as possible.

But if she came too soon, it was never a problem. She could always come again. And again. And again.

"I want you inside me," she said, her voice ragged and soft.

"Not yet," he whispered.

"Now," she demanded, tugging at his shoulders, struggling to get out of his grasp.

He smiled up at her. "Impatient thing, aren't you?"

"You're killing me." Her forehead was glazed with perspiration, and he could feel the dampness at the base of her back, too, where she always got wet right before she came.

Marc urged her down on the floor next to him, and she eagerly complied. Then he tugged her top off, turned her around and leaned her over the cushioned desk chair. The sight of her slender smooth back made his dick harder, and he leaned down and kissed her there as he freed himself from his fly.

He found a condom in his pocket that he'd placed there that morning for just such an occasion. He tore it open with his teeth, sheathed himself and pushed into her.

She felt like melting butter, so soft and smooth it nearly brought tears to his eyes. Her warmth enveloped him and made him want to push deeper and deeper still.

He wanted her too much. It wasn't sane to want a woman more than anything else. It wasn't safe, either. It meant he was vulnerable to all sorts of things he didn't want to be vulnerable to. He was capable of losing his bearings and the life he'd planned for himself.

But for an adventurer like himself, wasn't planning his life out equally unwise?

Marc pushed the unwanted thoughts aside as he began moving in her, his body tense from pleasure.

He wanted to obliterate their every worry, their every care, with each thrust. He wanted to lose himself in her and never come back to reality.

As the tension of an orgasm built inside of him, he could only hope that in facing his greatest desire and his greatest peril in Ariel, he would survive to tell the tale.

14

"What's Love Got to Do With It?"

Sorry, cliché title, I know, but have you ever listened to Tina Turner's song? I mean, really listened?

It's profound stuff.

Love may intensify our ability to experience pleasure, but it also increases our chances of feeling pain—often excruciating pain.

Is it worth the trade-off? Well? Is it?

I think not. And Tina Turner didn't think so, either.

Like she so aptly said, it's a secondhand emotion. She'd been burned, and she knew of what she sang. So why do we continually take the risk?

Is it so wrong that I live my life avoiding burn marks?

Comments:
1. juju says: Not wrong at all. Cowardly, but not wrong.

2. NOLAgirl says: We keep taking the risks because we're hardwired to want love. Survival of the species and all that.

3. Asiana says: What's going on, Eurogirl? I'm sensing our intrepid heroine is dealing with some messy emotional stuff sullying her fabulous sex life.

MARC SAT DOWN at the bar beside Nicholas Kozowski. He felt as if he'd known the man forever, but in reality, he'd only met Nicholas in his training days when he'd been a cocky young recruit who thought he knew everything.

The only thing that had changed was that now, he understood how little he really knew. Life and the endless challenges of being an operative had taught him humility, among other things.

"Thank you for making a special trip up here just to see me," Marc said.

"Don't flatter yourself. I just wanted to visit Bellagio again."

"Already done with your business in Rome?"

The older man nodded, his usual private self, never giving away an unnecessary detail.

"I'm on my way to Munich next."

"It's good to see you, even if just for a drink." Marc ordered a Heineken from the bartender.

"You look tired," Nicholas said.

The guy was one to talk. His sixty-eight years showed in his eyes, in the leathery tan of his skin and in the shock of gray hair that hung over his brow. He was old-school, and he'd survived situations that would have driven lesser men insane.

Marc shrugged. "Maybe I am."

"You're a little young to be sounding so jaded. Give it another ten years and then you'll have a good reason to feel burned out." His tone was joking, but Marc could tell he was digging to see what was really going on.

"Don't think I haven't noticed how you look out for me. I appreciate it, but really, I'm not burned out."

At least, he didn't think he was....

"Oh? Then why did you drop the ball on your mission in Rome?"

Marc could feel his usual poker face give way to a moment of embarrassment. His first instinct was to protest. He hadn't dropped the ball. He'd followed every lead, and they'd all led exactly nowhere.

But...

Could he really say that honestly when he'd gotten so distracted by Ariel?

"I think I was given a lame-duck mission. There wasn't any imminent terrorist threat at the embassy."

Nicholas eyed him suspiciously. "Can you say that with absolute assuredness?"

"Yeah," Marc answered, but he didn't sound as sure as he'd hoped.

"You still love the job?"

"I'm not as endlessly eager to get the bad guys as I used to be," Marc said.

Nicholas nodded solemnly. Marc couldn't describe a feeling or situation the older man hadn't already felt or been through. And he was very tempted to describe the situation with Ariel, to admit that he was falling in love with a woman he was supposed to be investigating and protecting, but saying it aloud felt too much like making it real.

And he wasn't sure he was ready to admit to himself that it was real.

"You've been on this assignment for four years. Maybe it's time to start a new one."

"I've thought about that," Marc said, a sick feeling settling in his gut. "Maybe you're right."

"There's a danger in staying in one place too long—you get stale, you establish too many roots and you don't want to move on."

Marc nodded. "Tell me about it."

"Is there, perhaps, a woman you're wanting to get away from?"

"Probably more than one," Marc joked, but Nicholas had skirted too close to the truth.

He didn't want to leave because of Ariel, but given the intensity between them, he knew they were destined to crash hard and burn out fast. He'd been there before, and he had the scars to prove it. Leaving before the crash sounded like a sane choice.

"I heard about the angry ex making a scene at the embassy," Nicholas said.

Marc winced. "Yeah, nice, huh? You know you're

in trouble when the women you've been with are your worst enemies."

"Is that it? No other woman troubles to speak of?"

"Have you heard anything else?"

Nicholas's face gave away nothing, but Marc knew his mentor well enough to know he definitely had heard more. "The woman in the terrorist database, Ariel Turner—you're sleeping with her, right?"

He nodded. "I guess we've been doing quite a bit more than sleeping."

"I'd imagine so. I've seen her photo. Definitely your type."

"I don't have a type." But even as Marc protested, he realized he did. He went for dangerous, beautiful women, like a man drawn to toying with exotic predators.

"What do you know about her?"

"Her connection with the November 17 movement was purely coincidental far as I can tell."

"Far as you can tell, or far as your dick can?"

"Screw you, man."

"It's a danger of getting too close, as you know. You lose touch with the mission."

"I haven't gotten too close emotionally. Just physically."

"Yeah, and that's why you want to move on to a new assignment, right?"

"I didn't ask you here to bust my chops. I just wanted some friendly advice, maybe a little career guidance."

"What? Do I look like your freaking high school guidance counselor?"

Marc said nothing, feeling suddenly like a sullen teenager.

"You want career guidance? Here's a little tip—don't investigate with your dick. It's going to get you into bigger shit than you can handle."

"What exactly do you think I can't handle?"

"You'll know it when you get there, and by then it'll be too late."

"Cryptic warnings are always so helpful. Thanks a bunch."

"I know what you're going through only because I've been through it myself. You find yourself falling hard for this girl, and you're all screwed up in the head not knowing where the mission ends and your love life begins."

Marc shrugged. "Yeah, maybe."

"Here's a little hint. Your mission doesn't end. It's part of the job. You have to keep it separate from reality if you want to stay sane and have any chance of a half-assed normal life."

"There's no such thing as normal in our line of work. You know that."

"We wouldn't be in it if normal was what we wanted."

Nicholas was right, of course. Marc had always run away from the typical settle-down-and-raise-a-family life. He'd known he needed more than that. He'd wanted excitement and adventure.

Unfortunately, after ten years, what had been exciting had become the norm, and the truly edgy life seemed to be the opposite of what he had. He was beginning to see how it was all about perspective. And his, with his rejection of conformity, had gotten a wee bit skewed, to say the least.

"Did you ever get tired of this lifestyle and wish for something else?" Marc asked.

"Sure, don't we all? I came this close to retiring about ten times."

"What kept you from doing it?"

Nicholas sighed. "I knew I didn't have it in me to do something else."

"But? There's something you're not saying."

"I certainly had my moments when I wish I could have found it in me to settle down and all that."

"But you didn't."

"Hell, no."

"What made you wish?"

"A woman, of course, but I'm not going to talk about that now."

"I didn't mean for things to get out of hand with Ariel, but—"

"You don't get a choice sometimes. Some people come into our lives just to screw it up."

And some people came into their lives to do something more. Some people, Marc suspected, were there to teach, to love, to be a friend. Ariel freaked him out sometimes because it felt as if she was doing all three.

"Listen, man. I'll put in for you to transfer if you want. Just say the word."

Marc hesitated, then nodded. "Yeah. Go ahead. Send me as far away from Italy as you can get me. I need the change of scenery."

"You'll need to file a report on Ariel, you know," Nicholas said.

"She's clean. I swear."

"Doesn't matter what you swear. You need some solid proof, and you need to stop screwing her. Immediately."

Marc nodded and tried his best to look chastened, but he didn't exactly feel that way. He knew he wouldn't stop sleeping with her. "There's one more thing, though. I have to ask a favor of you."

"Shoot."

"Ariel's actually in trouble. Some guy's after her, probably the terrorist ex, and I need some resources to catch him."

"How do you plan to justify that?"

"If it is the ex, he had to have been involved in that November 17 attack in Athens a few years back. If I can catch him, I can hand him over to the Greek government to have their way with him."

Nicholas nodded. "Which might win us a few favors. Sounds like you've thought it through. Go ahead and use whatever extra resources you need."

"I owe you big-time. Thanks."

"Don't mention it. I'll be considering the best way for me to collect on the favor, so beware."

ARIEL SANK INTO the lounge chair as she gazed out at the placid lake. The setting sun's light danced off the gentle ripples in the water, creating one of a million postcard-perfect images she'd seen since arriving in Italy. It was a place of magic, cliché as that sounded. A place where beauty could be lived and breathed.

Part of her never wanted to leave, and another part of her felt a low-level sense of panic that never quite went away, even here in the safety of Bellagio, far away from all her real-world worries.

"Hey," she heard Marc's voice say from behind her.

He took a seat on the lounge next to her, and immediately she knew something was wrong.

"What is it?" she said.

"We need to talk."

"That's an ominous-sounding statement."

She could tell by the way he avoided eye contact, choosing instead to gaze out at the lake, that he didn't think she was going to like whatever he had to say.

"Last night, when you mentioned your blog?"

"Yes?" she said, a sick feeling settling in her stomach.

"There's something I need to confess to you."

Her mind raced to guess what it was. He had a wife? A fiancée? A bizarre fetish? Or even worse, had he been reading her blog?

"When I looked you up in the CIA database, it

also mentioned your identity as an anonymous blogger."

Ariel felt her jaw drop. That was what she'd been dreading he would say.

Then she recalled the post from Marco Polo, and she knew. "You've posted on my blog, haven't you?"

He nodded. "As Marco Polo. I guess that was my halfhearted attempt to let you know that I knew. Or something like that."

The truth kept sinking in, and the sick feeling in Ariel's stomach kept growing. She sat up in the lounge chair and stared at him as if she didn't know him. His face wasn't registering as the guy she'd actually started feeling things for, actually started trusting this past week.

Now he was the guy who'd invaded her last layer of defense.

"Why didn't you tell me?"

"I was investigating you at first, and by the time I knew you were clean, I could never find a time that felt right. And I couldn't stop reading your posts."

Her face burned, and she thought of what he would have been reading. Every damn thing she'd written about him. Every damn thing she'd written about all the other men she'd been with.

She was horrified, but why? He was a grown man with a sordid sexual history of his own, and she was a grown woman with strong opinions about sex. She should have been okay with the fact that he'd read her blog. But she felt violated, as if he'd taken a stroll inside her mind. He was getting too close and he knew her too well.

She tried to stand up, but he reached out and held her arm.

"Didn't it make you feel weird, reading all that stuff?"

Marc nodded. "Sure, at first. And I got really jealous of all the other men you'd written about."

"Jealous?"

"I hated thinking of you with them, doing things you'd done with me." He shrugged. "I'm a guy, after all. I have a male ego."

Ariel's head started spinning. Or at least her thoughts did. They became a jumble of emotions and words that made no sense, and she felt her anger becoming fury. Because she was embarrassed. Because she'd been fooled and violated.

"I was writing anonymously! I wasn't writing for people who know who I am!"

"You post that stuff in a public forum, Ariel. What the hell do you expect? Sooner or later someone will find out who you are. It's not hard to do."

"I expected you to be honest with me, not lie about how much you knew."

His expression softened. "I'm very sorry. I know I should have told you up front."

"But you didn't."

"I had all sorts of rationalizations, like that I could be a better lover to you by studying what you like, that I could get to know you more intimately when you were unwilling to let me get closer to you the regular way."

Ariel shrugged his hand from her arm and stood up. Now she understood why he'd felt so perfect for her—not because he was, but because he'd concocted an act based on what he thought she wanted. It had been bullshit, every minute of their time together.

"I don't want to stay here." She needed to get as far away from him as she could, as fast as she could.

"Ariel, please. Be practical if nothing else. We need to keep you safe, first and foremost."

"I'll just leave the country. I don't have to stay here anymore. I can go back to the U.S. early."

As soon as the words left her mouth, she knew it was what she wanted to do.

Finally she had no reason to stay in Europe, and every reason in the world to go home.

Home. It wasn't a physical place anymore, but she knew where her home was. It was where she was loved unconditionally. She would go back to her brother, help him with his wedding and be his family in a real way again.

"Ariel, please don't go." Marc stood up, too.

But she had no intention of believing anything else he said, ever again. He'd lied about one thing, then another and another. Three strikes, and he was out of her life for good.

She was no fool. Or at least she would be one no longer.

"I'll take a taxi to the train station. Don't try to stop me."

"I can't let you do this."

"You don't have any choice, Marc. You're not my babysitter."

"What about Kostas?"

"I'll go back to the U.S. Now that the authorities are looking for him, he can't follow me and there's no reason for me to stay here any longer."

She turned and went into the house, letting the door slam behind her.

15

"What's Love Got to Do With It?"

Comments Continued...
4. lala says: Eurogirl, love has NOTHING to do with it.

5. tokyolover says: I think I'm hardwired to want sushi, not love.

6. dharmachick says: Eurogirl, just remember, there isn't much point in anything unless we have people who love us and drive us crazy. Love is what separates us from the ants.

THERE WAS A FLIGHT LEAVING Rome for the U.S. the next morning, Ariel discovered when she called her travel agent. Within twenty minutes, she'd booked the flight for herself and the cat and made arrangements for transportation to and from the airports.

Then she called her landlord and explained the situation, apologizing that she would have to so quickly vacate her room and letting her know she would be happy to pay extra on top of the deposit to make up for Fabiana's trouble—not to mention the burden of adopting Ariel's cat. The older woman refused any further money, but Ariel made a mental note to leave something extra regardless.

Her final call was to the family that had employed her. She hated being so flaky, disappearing from the job as soon as she'd started, but there was no way around it now. She referred them to another tutor she knew who was looking for work, and that eased her conscience a bit.

With her ties to Italy so quickly broken and her travel arrangements made, she had only her brother left to call, but she didn't want to deal with his nosy questions right now. She'd save that call for the airport, or some other time when she was feeling fortified enough to explain everything.

Now all she had to do was sit back on the train and wait for it to depart.

Ariel stared out the window at the darkness and tried to ignore the sick feeling in her stomach. But ignoring it wasn't working. It was getting worse, the farther she got from Marc.

There wasn't any other way, though. She could stay and let herself get crushed by inevitable heartbreak, or she could cut loose from the relationship now and feel heartbroken, but not as badly as it would feel later, when she'd gotten even more lost in her feelings.

Her stupid, unrealistic feelings.

This was why she'd lived her life free of commitments. This was exactly the kind of thing she'd been hoping to avoid. Blistering, unrestrained pain of the worst kind. She'd had enough of it as a kid, watching her parents self-destruct, and she'd had more than enough of it trying to raise her brother and watching him nearly self-destruct himself.

She'd spent her adult life running away from this very feeling, she realized now. And she didn't think it had been such a bad idea.

The train finally left the station at nightfall.

Ariel gave up any hope of glimpsing scenery in the darkness and closed her eyes, wrapping her arms around herself as she rested her head against the back of the seat.

The sound of the train lulled her, and she didn't wake up until it had stopped in Rome. Ariel blinked at the light in the station, yawned and stretched. Around her, the bustle of passengers exiting created a din, and she stood up to join them, grabbing her bags from the overhead bin as she went.

But when she stepped off the train, a hand grabbed her arm and she found Kostas next to her.

"I have a gun pointed at your side, so do not make a sound or give away any hint that you don't want to be with me. Do you understand?"

Ariel's mouth went dry, and she immediately understood just how stupid she'd been to leave Bellagio. She'd voluntarily walked right into this.

She was a fool.

A much bigger fool than she or Marc had even realized.

"I understand," she finally whispered as he dragged her along. "Where are you taking me?"

"You have your passport?"

"Yes."

"We're going back to Athens, where you will be asked some questions and persuaded to answer truthfully and completely."

"You don't have to take me all the way there. I can be honest with you right here, right now."

Panic had now seized her chest, and she was having a hard time breathing. She desperately wanted to break away from him and run, but she suspected it wouldn't be hard for him to shoot her dead and disappear into the crowd.

"Don't take me for a fool, Ariel."

"I—" He cut her short by jabbing the gun into her rib cage, sending a slicing pain through her side. She grunted at it and almost tripped as he tugged at her arm.

"You're going to proceed with me to the next train and you will behave like we're lovers getting along just fine. No funny business, or I will shoot."

Ariel believed him. He'd probably been threatened with death himself by his superiors if he didn't take care of her, so he would have nothing to lose by risking capture to deal with her.

He guided her past five or six platforms before they reached another train to board. Its destination was the port of Venice. So that meant they were probably taking a boat back to Athens. A private boat? Where he could throw her overboard when he was done with her?

Ariel's throat seized up.

She had to keep her head straight and think. She had to find a way to escape before they reached the coast. She didn't want to die, and she especially didn't want to die by drowning in the middle of the ocean, left for shark bait.

Five minutes later, they were in a private sleeper compartment of a train, and Ariel still hadn't thought of any solution that wouldn't be utterly and completely obvious to Kostas. He sat beside her, nervously bobbing his knee as they waited for the train to depart.

Ariel's only hope was that he hadn't searched her. She had her cell phone in her pocket, and he didn't even know she'd gotten a cell phone since coming to Italy. For once in her life, her technophobe tendencies might turn out to be a good thing…if she got lucky. She still had to find a moment alone to use the phone.

"I'm going to need to use the restroom," she said, hoping she still might find a way to slip off the train before it left the station.

"We'll go together when the train is moving. I don't want you looking for any little windows of escape," he said, and Ariel's heart sank.

She decided to take a different tack. If she could

lull him into thinking she didn't want to get away, maybe he'd relax a bit. Okay, so it sounded like something someone in a bad made-for-TV movie would try, but that basically described her entire life right now, didn't it?

She looked out the window as passengers hurried through the station, dragging bags behind them, glancing at watches, reading signs. They were all caught up in their own lives, unaware of the crazed terrorist with a loaded gun sitting next to her right now, holding her captive.

Time seemed to be moving like molasses, creeping forward so slowly it couldn't be felt. She shifted in her seat, her heart still racing, and tried to focus on breathing in and out slowly, tried to calm herself down a little.

She'd need a calm, clear head to find a way out of this.

Kostas's phone rang as they were pulling out of the station, and he answered it with his free hand, speaking Greek to the person on the line. Ariel understood enough to catch most of his conversation, which was brief, and seemed to be about her. He said that he'd found her, and that he was on his way and that there had been no problems. As he spoke, he watched her with vaguely hostile eyes.

She looked away and tried not to seem bothered by his hostility. When he hung up the phone, she swallowed her terror and forced herself to speak calmly.

"I never said so, but I'm sorry I left without any explanation," she said.

He cast her a wary glance. "I'll bet you are."

"I never lied about my feelings, and I cared about you. I thought we were more than just casual lovers."

Kostas smiled. "I thought we were extraordinary lovers, myself."

And they had been. "I wouldn't have stuck around for so long if not."

Something about his posture shifted from hostile to relaxed. It never failed—compliment a guy on his sexual prowess and he couldn't help but believe it. Guys were just wired that way.

A conductor passed by and took two tickets from Kostas, then moved on to the next car.

Ariel's sense of panic was growing rather than subsiding. She knew her chances of escaping would be nonexistent if she had to board a boat with Kostas, and she knew she might only get one chance to get away.

And she might die trying.

She didn't want to die. She thought of Marc, and of the way he'd made her feel. It was an entirely different kind of relationship than what she'd had with Kostas or any of the other men she'd been with. It was deeper, more intricate and far more emotional. She'd wanted so badly to keep emotion out of it, and the opposite had happened.

She'd probably been right to try to avoid the emotional entanglement and she'd been wrong to trust Marc when he'd given every sign he wasn't trustworthy, but she couldn't get him out of her head.

She'd been around the block enough times to know what that meant.

Love.

She'd started falling into it, and now she'd have to crawl bleeding back out of that particular pit.

That is, if she lived long enough to do so. She could still feel the presence of the gun in Kostas's pocket, barely brushing her side, but he'd relaxed a bit, and she could only hope that her window of opportunity was cracking open the tiniest bit.

"I really need to use the restroom now," she said, pretending to shift uncomfortably in her seat.

"Okay, but if you try anything, it will be the last thing you try. Do you understand?"

She nodded.

"I'll follow you, and I'll wait outside your door."

Ariel's breath caught in her throat, and she forced herself to breathe steadily again. In, out, in, out...

She followed the signs to the restroom, and when she'd closed the door of the tiny compartment and locked it, she pulled her cell phone out of her pocket and started a new text message. She couldn't risk Kostas hearing her talk, but she could text Marc silently.

With her hands trembling so badly she could barely hit the buttons correctly, she keyed in the message, N trouble, on train 5233 2 Venice. Need help. With Kostas. Arriving 9:25 p.m. Please find me before then.

She selected his phone number and hit Send, then flushed the toilet and washed her hands. Before leaving the restroom, she set her phone to silent mode and tucked it into the side of her panties, where she hoped Kostas wouldn't discover it.

Ariel tried to appear calm as she came back out to face Kostas, and by his blasé expression, she realized she just might have gotten away with it. He didn't know what she'd done. And maybe, if she was lucky, she'd just saved herself.

HE'D BEEN A FOOL to let her go. He should have been more persuasive, more forceful, more something. Less of a dumb-ass.

He never should have let his emotions get involved, because that's what had been their undoing, and if she died now, he would have no one but himself to blame.

Marc vowed not to let it happen again. Regardless of any pain it caused him, he'd keep his feelings to himself with regard to Ariel from here on out. He wouldn't allow her to be endangered under his watch again.

The weight of the cell phone in his pocket nagged at him now, reminding him of his ex-girlfriend, of her anger, of the anger of all the women who'd come before her.

Some part of him had wanted things with Ariel

to go differently. He'd wanted it not to end with bad feelings.

He'd wanted her not to hate him.

He'd been a fool.

Maybe it was better this way. At least there was no doubt about his true character. And she wouldn't have to wonder what might have been.

It was easier to move on from anger, wasn't it?

Marc hoped like hell it was, because he could already tell it was going to be hell to move on from the pain of a broken heart.

The text message kept repeating itself in his head as he sped through the mountains toward the coast. He'd called in help to stop the train, alerting authorities to Kostas's identity and physical description, but he couldn't help fearing that the *Carabinieri* would screw up and Ariel would end up dead because of it.

He couldn't let that happen.

And he didn't want to examine why he felt so desperate not knowing if she was safe.

No more going there.

The Italian countryside went by in a blur. He received a call from a colleague that the train would be stopped one station before its final destination, where the *Carabinieri* would hold Kostas until Marc or another operative could arrive. There was someone closer to the town than Marc, but he raced ahead nonetheless, wanting to be there to see for himself that Ariel was okay.

He could only hope....

After three hours on a road that would have taken five if he'd been driving the speed limit, he arrived at the small-town train station only minutes after the train had been scheduled to arrive.

His gut twisted when he spotted the number of the train Ariel was—or had been—on, and he ran across the parking lot, spotting the *Carabinieri* as he rounded the side of the train. First he saw a tall, dark-haired man in handcuffs, escorted by a CIA operative he recognized and then, his gaze roaming the crowd, he found Ariel standing off to the side talking to a man in a police uniform.

Her face was tear streaked, but she was alive.

She was okay. No thanks to him.

He pushed through the crowd as Kostas was being led away, arriving at Ariel's side just as she was turning away from the officer. Her gaze landed on him and she looked surprised.

"You got the message," she said. "Thank you."

"Ariel, I'm sorry. I never should have let you go."

She shook her head. "No, it's totally my fault. I walked right into this danger and I have no one but myself to blame."

"Thank God you were able to text me."

"He didn't know I had a phone with me," she said, glancing in the direction of her ex-boyfriend, who was being taken out of the station now.

Marc wanted to reach out and grab her, pull her to him and hold her tight and kiss her like there was no tomorrow, but he knew the time for that has passed. He knew there would be no more indulging in his physical desires, or his emotional ones, not when doing so had brought her so close to such danger.

For once in his life, he'd have some restraint. Even if it was a little late in coming.

Ariel deserved that from him, at the very least.

"I'm glad you're safe," he said lamely. "You'll need to answer some questions from an interviewer, but after that you'll be free to go…back to the U.S. if you want."

She nodded. "I already talked to the CIA guy."

"Oh. I guess you're all done here, then."

"I'm sorry I left angry," she said. "I'm not mad anymore. I know it's for the best that we end things now."

"Right," he said, feeling as if he'd been kicked in the gut.

Ariel smiled, but it looked forced. "We knew we'd crash and burn from the start, didn't we?"

Marc met her gaze but said nothing. The truth was too ugly to face right now.

"It's okay. We are who we are. You're a player, I'm a player. It's in our nature not to settle down."

"You're right," he said, sounding more sure of himself than he felt.

But he would be strong this time. He'd let her go before she got hurt for real.

She leaned forward and placed a soft kiss on his lips—so soft, it almost wasn't there.

And then, without saying goodbye and without looking back, she turned and walked away.

16

"What's Love Got to Do With It?"

Comments Continued...
7. timberwolf says: Eurogirl, where are you? Did you get lost in love or something.

8. juju says: timberwolf, dude, I think that's the most romantic thing you've ever said.

9. dharmachick says: Seriously, Eurogirl, we're worried about you. Could you at least check in and let us know you didn't die in a freak gondola accident or something?

10. emmy says: C'mon, people, every other time Eurogirl has ever disappeared from her blog, we all know what she's been doing. Getting laid, unlike some of us.

THE ITALIAN COUNTRYSIDE passed by in endlessly beautiful scenes. As he drove, Marc watched it all as if it wasn't there. He saw, but he didn't see. Beside him, Nicholas sighed noisily and closed the *Herald Tribune* he'd been reading.

"Are you going to spend all damn day looking like that? Because I don't think I can be in this car with you if you are. You're depressing the hell out of me."

Marc blinked at him. "What?"

"Cheer up, man."

He turned his attention back to driving and said nothing. He should have taken Ariel's departure as just another breakup, but it didn't feel like the rest. The car rounded a bend in a hillside, and a picturesque Tuscan field spread into the distance in all its golden glory.

Nicholas had finished his business in Munich early, and he'd called Marc to meet him in Florence for a trip to Turin, where they would arrange Marc's next assignment.

The older man sighed again. "Look, some women are worth giving it all up for. A few of them, anyway."

"You're not giving me advice on women, are you?"

"You look like you need it."

"What I need is to get the hell out of Italy. I thought that's what you were going to help me with."

"You didn't stop screwing that girl like I told you to, did you?"

"She went back to the U.S. I definitely stopped screwing her."

"Only because she left."

"You're not one to be giving advice, you know. I've heard your track record. You're probably the only guy I know who's more screwed up than me."

"Consider me a cautionary tale."

"You really believe some women are worth giving up your freedom and everything else that matters to you?"

"Ask yourself, what *really* matters to you, anyway?"

"Weren't you the one telling me a week ago to stay the hell away from her?"

"I can tell your heart's not in the job anymore."

Marc opened his mouth to spout and answer, but nothing emerged. The truth, he feared, was that everything had stopped mattering when Ariel left.

"I met one of those women once, the kind worth giving it all up for, and I was a fool. I gave *her* up instead of the crap that didn't matter. I've always regretted it, and I've always wondered what might have been."

Marc felt as if he'd been kicked in the stomach. He would spend his life wondering what might have been with Ariel. He knew he would.

"Why'd you do it?"

"Same reason you let your girl walk away. I was scared as hell."

"I'm not scared," Marc said, but the words rang false in his own ears.

He was scared. As hell. Afraid of how vulnerable love could make him, afraid of how much power

Ariel could wield over him, afraid of giving up the life he knew for one he didn't know.

"I'm just saying, don't be a coward. It's no way to live your life."

Marc had never thought of himself as a coward. He lived his life on the edge, and he faced dangers most men would never know, but maybe... Maybe when it came to the dangers of the heart, he had never been forced to exhibit any kind of bravery.

Or maybe when it came to such matters, he had no bravery to exhibit.

Back in the USA
I set foot back on U.S. soil again for the first time in five years this morning. The first thing I noticed was the scent of fast food wafting out of a nearby airport restaurant—a greasy scent like no other. Then I noticed the people, ninety percent of whom had the unmistakable look of America.

We're a nation full of ease and excess, and it shows in our open, friendly faces, our expensive name-brand sneakers and our constant dissatisfaction with what we have.

We're always wanting more, which is an idea I contemplated on my cab ride to my brother's house, where I will be staying until I find a place of my own again.

Had that philosophy of always wanting more somehow invaded my bedroom, taken over my love life? Had I become the ugly American of sex?

I returned home chastened by my experiences, I'm chagrined to say. There is no simple happy ending to my years spent sexing my way around Europe. I lived, and what I learned was that I wasn't really satisfied with just living. I wanted love, too.

Maybe I didn't find it, but at least I found my desire for it. And that's something, right?

Here I am sounding all morose. That's not the feeling I want to convey. But how to explain that the feeling of always wanting more is not a healthy thing, while at the same time admitting that I did indeed discover a desire for something more than I've been chasing after all these years?

I don't have all the answers. I don't even have one of the answers. I only know that I'm ready to be here, back in America, starting the next phase of my life.

It's no longer a quest for the perfect lover. It is, cliché as it may sound, a quest for the perfect love.

Ariel stared at the blog entry she'd drafted, chewing her lip as she debated whether or not to post it. There was so much pressure in coming up with the right "back in America" post. So much to say, and so much she didn't want to say. But her blog had always been a spontaneous and fairly honest place. She laid it all bare online, and she didn't know why she was so hesitant to be naked and honest there now.

Maybe there was no way to tell the whole truth

about her time in Europe. Maybe there was no way to sum up all her conflicting feelings in one neat little post. Maybe she would need a whole series of posts.

She saved the draft and closed the Web browser, deciding not to publish the post for the time being. She'd think about it overnight.

"Are you ever going to get off of that damn computer and help me with the reception favors?" Trey asked, standing beside her.

He had one hand on his hip, and the other hand held a small, sheer iridescent lavender sack that had a satin drawstring. Inside the bag were some smooth stones and white shells.

"What's that?" Ariel asked.

"The reception favors. Every guest gets a little bag of rocks and seashells."

"To throw at you as you leave for your honeymoon? That's original."

"Yes, we've arranged to be stoned by the mob as we exit our gay wedding. That's exactly the idea. It's what all the hip gay couples are doing these days."

She smiled. "Aren't you afraid some people will think that's what they're supposed to do with the rocks?"

"If we have friends who are that stupid, then we deserve to be pelted with rocks."

"Hey, don't forget there might be some family members in attendance."

Trey winced. "Maybe on Devan's side, but not ours."

"Not even Aunt Lenore RSVP'd yes?"

"It's the location. She couldn't afford a trip to Hawaii."

"You planned it that way, didn't you?"

"I admit to no such strategy."

"You don't have to admit to it," Ariel said as she closed her laptop and set it aside.

They may have been joking around, but she knew the whole family issue was a more sensitive subject than Trey was willing to admit.

She wished she could think of a way to broach it without making him feel like shit.

"Okay, so how do I help?"

"I've got the stuffing station set up on the dining room table," he said, leading her into the dining room.

"The stuffing station?"

"We have about two hundred of these little bags to stuff."

"Did you say two hundred?"

He looked at her like she was stupid. "One for every guest."

"God, Trey, did you invite everyone you know?"

"I have lots of gay friends, okay? They love attending weddings, and I couldn't exclude anyone without risking huge drama and never getting invited to their wedding in turn."

"Why is it only heterosexuals hate weddings these days?"

"Because they're not novel to you anymore. You've been saddled with the convention from the dawn of time, whereas we gays are all giddy with the chance to join in the party finally."

He took a seat on one side of the table and Ariel sat down across from him. In the middle of the table were boxes of shells and rocks, all shiny and clean and ready for use in weddings and other sterile occasions, and a box full of the little purple bags.

"So, we're doing about five rocks and three shells per bag, plus one of these little slips of paper in each bag," he said, pointing to a stack of small cream-colored fortune-cookie-message-sized papers Ariel hadn't noticed before.

"And people will want bags of rocks and stuff because?"

Trey rolled his eyes, growing more impatient by the second at her stupidity. "It's supposed to allow the guests to go home and create their own Zen gardens."

"Oh."

"Don't give me that condescending tone."

She picked up one of the slips of paper and read it.

A Zen Garden for You With Love from Trey and Devan.

She tried not to smile, because it definitely would have been interpreted as condescending.

"I know, you spend a few years in Europe and all of a sudden you think you're too good for us California provincial types."

"I'm just going through a little culture shock, that's all."

"You grew up here!"

"Five years away from all the vegetarian cuisine and Zen gardens and ridiculous excess is, believe it or not, a recipe for culture shock upon my return."

Trey's crisp white oxford contrasting with his tan and his golden blond hair in the afternoon light from the window, gave him a startling resemblance to their mother. Ariel felt a pang of sadness that their parents would never know or appreciate what a glorious person their son had become. She wasn't even sure they would have had the sense to appreciate him.

Perhaps it was better that they were no longer alive then. She didn't want her little brother's big day marred by sadness.

But he was way ahead of her. "What?" he demanded. "You're looking all morose. You don't like the little message papers? Too tacky?"

"No, not at all," she said, shaking her head. "I was just thinking of Mom and Dad."

His suspicious expression disappeared instantly. "Don't," he said gently.

But it was too late now. She'd already brought up the subject they so often avoided.

"They would have been happy for you," she said even though she wasn't sure it was true.

"You don't have to say that. We both know they were freaked out by me."

"People can learn and grow. I think they would have."

He shook his head, looking wistful. "It doesn't

matter, because I always knew you were the one who'd take care of me no matter what."

"You did?" She felt tears prickling her eyelids and she blinked them away.

"Of course I did. You were always my rock—pardon the pun. You were always there doing everything they were supposed to do."

Ariel hadn't been sure he'd ever noticed, and she felt a huge lump of guilt in her chest for the fact that as soon as she'd gotten the chance, she'd run away from him. She'd run off to Europe and left him behind.

"Now let's talk about something truly interesting, like the fact that I'm horny as hell."

"Do I really want to be having this conversation with you?"

"Devan had the bright idea that we should stop having sex for a month before the wedding so that our big night could be all the more exciting."

"Sounds like a good idea."

"Sure, if I don't mind getting an erection every time my boxers brush me the wrong way. I'm going to have to stand up in front of all our friends and family on my wedding day with a raging, rock-hard boner. It's a brilliant idea."

She laughed at the bitter tone in his voice, and he scowled at her as he filled a little bag.

"I'm sorry," she said, filling a bag herself.

She was happy for her brother, but something was nagging at her. Not just the sadness of their par-

ents being gone, and not just the weirdness of returning to America, but something more.

Something named Marc. She'd gotten a glimpse
of another world with him. A world her brother had
entered, where true love and commitment were
attainable dreams. A world where, she was afraid,
now that she'd glimpsed it, she could no longer be
satisfied with anything else.

17

Love or Something Like It

My little brother is getting married, which is one of the reasons I returned to the U.S. when I did (rumors of my demise were indeed greatly exaggerated, people). I'll be his "best man" in the wedding, which you might think would mean I don't have to wear an awful bridesmaid dress, but you would be wrong. They had one made just for me.

All this wedding stuff, combined with my final weeks in Italy, has me thinking about this business of true love. How it makes people do crazy things, and say sacred vows and force their friends and family to dress up in hideously ugly lavender gowns.

I realized, before I left Rome, that the problem with sex as a casual act is that, in essence, it's a language of love. It's a way we communicate our desire for each other, and sometimes, that desire is more than just the physical sort.

Sometimes, we're communicating our desire to intertwine not just our bodies but our entire lives, and if we communicate that to a person who doesn't want the same thing, we're screwed.

Literally and figuratively.

No matter where in the world you go, no matter the culture, sex in any language means more than just sex.

It's complicated, and to treat it as any less than it is, well…creates problems, to say the least.

I keep thinking of X. Ever since I left Italy, he's been on my mind. And not just on my mind, but in my heart. I realize I fell in love with him, and I was too big a coward to face it, or say it or find out where it might lead.

So I ran away. I don't know if he'll ever read this, or if it will even matter to him now if he does, but I want him to know he wasn't just another lover to me.

He was so much more.

ARIEL WATCHED the computer as it published the final blog entry. Her stomach churned, and she wanted to erase it already. At the same time, if she left it up, Marc might someday see it.

It was a cowardly way to admit her feelings, but she knew she'd screwed up too badly to go crawling back to him now. So she was leaving it up to fate.

Maui, three months later…

ARIEL BLINKED BACK TEARS at the sight of her sweet little brother in a white tuxedo. There were so many times throughout their lives when she'd stayed up all night worrying about whether he'd even live to see adulthood, and now, here he was, her baby brother, beaming and happy and about to get married.

She'd worried about and tried to take care of him through his childhood, his teen years of being picked on and beaten up, through his sexual experimentations and his heroin addiction. Somehow, they'd both survived it all.

And here they were. Trey was happy. He was a grown man she was immensely proud to call her brother. While Ariel was not happy, but at least she was somewhere along the road to self-realization. She'd had her stops and starts, but writing her book gave her a sense of purpose she'd never had before.

"Deep in thought?" a male voice asked, and Ariel turned to find Trey standing beside her, adjusting his corsage.

"I'm just having a proud big sister moment."

"You're not going to get all sappy and sentimental on me, are you?"

"I thought you loved sappy and sentimental." Ariel made a final adjustment to his corsage for him—roses that had been dyed lavender.

"I do, but I can't make it through this ceremony if you're standing behind me bawling."

She blinked back some more tears. "I won't cry, I promise."

Trey hugged her. "Oh, big sister, what am I going to do with you?"

"I'm just proud of you—that's all."

He regarded her seriously. "I'm alive today because of you, you know."

She shook her head, fighting back the damn tears.

But then Trey started crying, and there was no turning back. In a matter of seconds, Ariel's twenty-minute makeup job was wrecked.

"Just shut up," she said halfheartedly.

"No. You were the only person in the world who loved me and took care of me for a long time, and I want you to know your love didn't go unnoticed. I'm sorry I made things so hard on you."

Ariel bit her lip. She hadn't realized how badly she'd needed to hear that. "Thank you," she said.

"I know I wouldn't be here if it wasn't for you."

"You're my family," she whispered. "I think we kept each other alive. You gave me a purpose."

He wiped at his damp eyes. "But you ran away to Europe first chance you got."

He'd never brought that up aloud before. There had always been a tension between them, a silent acknowledgment that he was a big part of the reason she'd needed to run away, to leave the country, to get as far away from her responsibilities as she could.

"I still loved you. I just couldn't take the weight of responsibility anymore. Once I saw that you were going to be okay, I just felt this profound need to leave my old life behind."

"I missed you," he said.

"I missed you, too. It's good to be living near you again."

"You don't resent me?"

"I never did."

He blinked away more tears and hugged her again. Ariel took a deep breath, inhaling his scent of Calvin Klein cologne and said a silent prayer of thanks that her little brother was all grown-up and happy now.

"Are we finished being sappy?" she asked.

He smiled. "Definitely. Are you ready to walk me down the aisle?"

"Definitely."

They stepped out of the clubhouse when the music began, and a gentle ocean breeze greeted them. Trey and Devan had both wanted to walk down the aisle. First came Trey, escorted by Ariel, then Devan's "bridesmaids," and finally Devan escorted by his parents.

Ariel hoped it wasn't painful for Trey to see his partner's parents there for him when hers and Trey's were not, but she knew it was a pain he'd gotten used to. It was a pain that had made them both who they were.

She held his hand tightly as they passed by the audience seated in white chairs under the canopy of palm trees, and when they reached the altar, she kissed his cheek and took her place beside him while they watched Devan and his parents follow.

But Ariel's gaze landed on a familiar figure in

the last aisle. Long dark hair, beard, eyes hidden by dark glasses…Marc.

Her breath caught in her throat and her stomach did a whirl.

Marc.

What was he doing here, in Hawaii, at her brother's wedding?

His gaze was locked on her, and he raised his glasses to make sure she knew it. There was warmth and emotion in his eyes. And she felt tears welling up in hers all over again.

HE COULD NOT TAKE his gaze off her. She glowed with a beauty even greater than he'd remembered. Something about her had changed in the time they'd been apart. Perhaps it was an air of calm, of being settled in a way she'd never been in Italy. He hoped it wasn't just being away from him that had changed her.

He never wanted to spend another day apart from her, let alone another month. Not another minute.

Marc watched as Ariel stood in the receiving line at the reception. He'd slipped out of the ceremony ahead of all the other guests, not ready to face her yet. He needed to choose his moment well—at a time when they could talk without interruption. And he needed to work up the nerve to face her again and offer himself to her without qualifications, to lay his heart bare and expose it to the ultimate pleasure or pain.

He was finally ready.

Her gaze searched the room, but she couldn't see

him, and he was both surprised and thrilled to see what looked like disappointment on her face. But when the receiving line was done, the first dance began and she turned her attention to watching her brother and his partner, while Marc watched her.

He was ready to stop being the person who watched, and start just living.

When the second song began, and the dance floor filled with couples, Marc knew it was time. He slipped out of the shadows and found his way to her, where she stood alone looking wistful.

"May I have this dance?"

Ariel turned to him, and she smiled. "You. How did you—when did you—"

He held a finger to her lips. "I have my sources."

She allowed him to lead her onto the dance floor, where an R & B love song had couples slow-dancing. He slipped his arms around her and held her close as they swayed to the music.

"When you left Italy," he said, "I realized I'd been living my life for all the wrong reasons."

His throat tightened. He'd never rehearsed what he would say when he finally had her face-to-face with him. He'd just trusted that his heart would guide his words, but he hadn't realized how much emotion would well up and try to escape.

Ariel looked at him as if he'd just spoken a foreign language. "What are the right reasons?"

"Having someone to love. Having someone to make sacrifices for, someone to come home to."

She looked as if she wanted to argue with him for a moment, but then the expression passed, and she said simply, "Yeah."

"I don't want us to be apart again," he admitted, feeling as if he were stripping himself naked right there on the dance floor.

"But what about your work? Isn't it pretty much required that we'll be apart a lot?"

"I turned in my resignation papers."

He watched shock register on her face.

"You…resigned?"

Marc nodded.

"Why?"

"I don't want that to be my life anymore. Your leaving forced me to ask myself some hard questions, like whether I was avoiding commitment because of my career, or if I became a CIA agent so I could avoid commitment."

Ariel blinked at him, her gaze steady but tentative.

"I realized the job had always appealed to me mostly because it helped me avoid being committed to anyone or anything but the CIA. It kept me at a distance and I don't want to be that man anymore."

"Why?"

"I want you. I'm sorry I let you walk away," he said. "I should have told you before you left that you are the love of my life and that I don't want to live without you."

The words had come without warning, and now that he'd said them, now that they were hanging in the air with all that weight and meaning, he was surprised at how easy it had been, and how relieved he was to simply say what he felt.

If he got his heart broken now, at least he knew he'd given it his all.

But Ariel's eyes were leaking tears. She wiped at her face with the back of her hand as she watched him as if he might disappear at any moment.

"I love you, too," she said. "I was terrified of how much I love you. I ran away from it."

"Don't run away again," he said. "Please. Stay and give me a chance."

"I don't want to run anymore."

He believed her. She felt as if she was solidly in this moment, in this place, in his arms. Not going anywhere. He pulled her close and kissed her long and deep, and he knew, finally, that he had found his home.

Epilogue

Thailand, two years later…

ARIEL LET THE WARM OCEAN water lap at her feet, and closed her eyes, savoring the feel of it. A hand slipped around her waist, and she relaxed into Marc's embrace.

"Hey, you," he said. "It's midnight. What are you doing out here on the beach by yourself?"

"I was just thinking about stuff."

"Uh-oh. Thinking about stuff? That sounds dangerous."

She smiled. Marc knew her too well. When she started thinking about stuff, it generally meant he was in trouble. And lately, with their life together going well and her writing career finally starting to feel like a career as her book went into its second print run, she found herself looking around and thinking, what next?

This trip they'd made to Thailand with Trey and Devan seemed to be screaming the answer to that question for her.

"Do you ever miss the CIA?"

"Hell, no," he said.

A breeze stirred her nightgown, but the air was so thick with humidity, that it felt more like warm water washing over her.

"You're really happy being a writer?"

"Absolutely. I never would have had the guts to go for it if it hadn't been for you, you know."

Ariel felt some of the tension drain from her shoulders. She'd always harbored a little guilt that Marc had given up his CIA career for her. It had seemed such an essential part of him when they'd first met that she'd taken a while to adjust to the new Marc, the one who stayed up into the early morning hours writing postmodern spy novels and spent his afternoons making lunch for her and making love with her and generally making her insanely happy.

Who was this dream guy she'd gotten so lucky to have? Did she even deserve him?

"Yeah, well, there's always the downside. Now I have to live with my jealousy."

"Jealousy?"

"Over the fact that your first book is selling better than my book. It sucks."

He laughed. "Yeah, well, you're by far the better writer. You can feel smug about the fact that quality always loses out to sensationalism."

"Whatever." She tried to look annoyed, but she wasn't feeling it.

Marc wrapped his arms around her and pulled her against his chest. "Is that really what's bothering you?"

"Actually, no. I was thinking about bigger stuff, I guess. Like Trey and Devan's little girl."

The beautiful, exquisitely perfect little girl, Nia, they had traveled here to adopt.

"What about her?"

"When we were at the orphanage yesterday? I just…I just…"

She couldn't say it. How to tell her ex-spy, ex-playboy boyfriend whom she'd virtually forced into settling down that she not only wanted to marry him, but that she wanted to deliver the ultimate death blow to his carefree ways?

"You want to adopt a child, too?"

She blinked at him in the moonlight. He didn't look appalled or afraid or anything. He was actually smiling at her.

"Yeah," she whispered, almost afraid to admit it to herself. "I do."

In the past two years she'd come full circle, from being a girl who couldn't even handle the thought of being responsible for a pet goldfish, to a truly settled, happy woman who…

Who wanted a child.

"I don't think we could have walked into that orphanage and left without thinking of it. I feel exactly the same."

Ariel stared at him, amazed. But she should have known it. They were so much alike, in so many ways, half the time she wondered if they shared a brain.

"Oh, thank God. I was so worried you'd hate the idea."

Marc leaned in and kissed her softly. "Maybe we should make ourselves official then, huh?"

"What do you mean?" She was almost afraid to ask.

"You know—get married."

Oh. *The shared brain thing strikes again.*

"Oh. Wow. Um, yeah, maybe we should."

He laughed. "Try not to sound so excited."

"I just never thought you cared about the official part." And she hadn't, either, but lately, she was starting to like the idea.

"I know how I feel, but I think it's about time we let the rest of the world know we're a permanent thing. Besides, it'll look good on the adoption paperwork, right?"

"Let's do it," she said, and she meant it. She was ready to do the committed-for-life thing. Really and truly ready.

He kissed her again, this time letting his tongue explore her while his hands roamed over the thin fabric of her nightgown. He squeezed her ass and pressed his erection against her belly.

"Come to bed," he whispered against her lips. "We've got some celebrating to do."

* * * * *

Look for Jamie Sobrato's next
Harlequin Blaze novel!
Coming in June 2007

Set in darkness beyond the ordinary world.
Passionate tales of life and death.
With characters' lives ruled by laws the everyday
world can't begin to imagine.

n●cturne

It's time to discover the Raintree trilogy....

New York Times bestselling author
LINDA HOWARD
brings you the dramatic first book
RAINTREE: INFERNO

The Ansara Wizards are rising and the Raintree
clan must rejoin the battle against their foes,
testing their powers, relationships and forcing
upon them lives they never could have imagined
before....

Turn the page for a sneak preview
of the captivating first book
in the Raintree trilogy,
RAINTREE: INFERNO by LINDA HOWARD
On sale April 25.

Dante Raintree stood with his arms crossed as he watched the woman on the monitor. The image was in black and white to better show details; color distracted the brain. He focused on her hands, watching every move she made, but what struck him most was how uncommonly *still* she was. She didn't fidget or play with her chips, or look around at the other players. She peeked once at her down card, then didn't touch it again, signaling for another hit by tapping a fingernail on the table. Just because she didn't seem to be paying attention to the other players, though, didn't mean she was as unaware as she seemed.

"What's her name?" Dante asked.

"Lorna Clay," replied his chief of security, Al Rayburn.

"At first I thought she was counting, but she doesn't pay enough attention."

"She's paying attention, all right," Dante murmured. "You just don't see her doing it." A card counter had to remember every card played. Supposedly counting cards was impossible with the number of decks used by the casinos, but there were those rare individuals who could calculate the odds even with multiple decks.

"I thought that, too," said Al. "But look at this piece of tape coming up. Someone she knows comes up to her and speaks, she looks around and starts chatting, completely misses the play of the people to her left—and doesn't look around even when the deal comes back to her, just taps that finger. And damn if she didn't win. Again."

Dante watched the tape, rewound it, watched it again. Then he watched it a third time. There had to be something he was missing, because he couldn't pick out a single giveaway.

"If she's cheating," Al said with something like respect, "she's the best I've ever seen."

"What does your gut say?"

Al scratched the side of his jaw, considering. Finally, he said, "If she isn't cheating, she's the luckiest person walking. She wins. Week in, week out, she wins. Never a huge amount, but I ran the numbers and she's into us for about five grand a week. Hell, boss, on her way out of the casino she'll stop by a slot machine, feed a dollar in and walk away with at least fifty. It's never the same machine, either. I've had her watched, I've had her followed, I've even looked for the same faces in the casino every time she's in here, and I can't find a common denominator."

"Is she here now?"

"She came in about a half hour ago. She's playing blackjack, as usual."

"Bring her to my office," Dante said, making a swift decision. "Don't make a scene."

"Got it," said Al, turning on his heel and leaving the security center.

Dante left, too, going up to his office. His face was calm. Normally he would leave it to Al to deal with a cheater, but he was curious. How was she doing it? There were a lot of bad cheaters, a few good ones, and every so often one would come along who was the stuff of which legends were made: the cheater who didn't get caught, even when people were alert and the camera was on him—or, in this case, her.

It was possible to simply be lucky, as most people understood luck. Chance could turn a habitual loser into a big-time winner. Casinos, in fact, thrived on that hope. But luck itself wasn't habitual, and he knew that what passed for luck was often something else: cheating. And there was the other kind of luck, the kind he himself possessed, but it depended not on chance but on who and what he was. He knew it was an innate power and not Dame Fortune's erratic smile. Since power like his was rare, the odds made it likely the woman he'd been watching was merely a very clever cheat.

Her skill could provide her with a very good living, he thought, doing some swift calculations in his head. Five grand a week equaled $260,000 a year, and that was just from his casino. She probably hit them all, careful to keep the numbers relatively low so she stayed under the radar.

He wondered how long she'd been taking him, how long she'd been winning a little here, a little there, before Al noticed.

The curtains were open on the wall-to-wall window in his office, giving the impression, when one first opened the door, of stepping out onto a covered balcony. The glazed window faced west, so he could catch the sunsets. The sun was low now, the sky painted in purple and gold. At his home in the mountains, most of the windows faced east, affording him views of the sunrise. Something in him needed both the greeting and the goodbye of the sun. He'd always been drawn to sunlight, maybe because fire was his element to call, to control.

He checked his internal time: four minutes until sundown. Without checking the sunrise tables every day, he knew exactly when the sun would slide behind the mountains. He didn't own an alarm clock. He didn't need one. He was so acutely attuned to the sun's position that he had only to check within himself to know the time. As for waking at a particular time, he was one of those people who could tell himself to wake at a certain time, and he did. That talent had nothing to do with being Raintree, so he didn't have to hide it; a lot of perfectly ordinary people had the same ability.

He had other talents and abilities, however, that did require careful shielding. The long days of summer instilled in him an almost sexual high, when he could feel contained power buzzing just beneath his skin. He had to be doubly careful not to cause candles to leap into flame just by his presence, or to start wildfires with a glance in the dry-as-tinder brush. He loved Reno; he didn't want to burn it down. He just felt so damn *alive* with all the sunshine pouring down that he wanted to let the energy pour through him instead of holding it inside.

This must be how his brother Gideon felt while pulling lightning, all that hot power searing through his muscles, his veins. They had this in common, the connection with raw power. All the members of the far-flung Raintree clan had some power, some heightened ability, but only members of the royal family could channel and control the earth's natural energies.

Dante wasn't just of the royal family, he was the Dranir, the leader of the entire clan. "Dranir" was synonymous with king, but the position he held wasn't ceremonial, it was one of sheer power. He was the oldest son of the previous Dranir, but he would have been passed over for the position if he hadn't also inherited the power to hold it.

Behind him came Al's distinctive knock on the door. The outer office was empty, Dante's secretary having gone home hours before. "Come in," he called, not turning from his view of the sunset.

The door opened, and Al said, "Mr. Raintree, this is Lorna Clay."

Dante turned and looked at the woman, all his senses on alert. The first thing he noticed was the vibrant color of her hair, a rich, dark red that encompassed a multitude of shades from copper to burgundy. The warm amber light danced along the iridescent strands, and he felt a hard tug of sheer lust in his gut. Looking at her hair was almost like looking at fire, and he had the same reaction.

The second thing he noticed was that she was spitting mad.

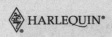

EVERLASTING LOVE™

Every great love has a story to tell™

If you're a romantic at heart, you'll definitely want to read this new series.

Available April 24

The Marriage Bed by Judith Arnold

An emotional story about a couple's love that is put to the test when the shocking truth of a long-buried secret comes to the surface.

&

Family Stories by Tessa McDermid

A couple's epic love story is pieced together by their granddaughter in time for their seventy-fifth anniversary.

And look for

The Scrapbook by Lynnette Kent

&

When Love Is True by Joan Kilby

from Harlequin® Everlasting Love™ this June.

Pick up a book today!

REQUEST YOUR FREE BOOKS!

2 FREE NOVELS
PLUS 2
FREE GIFTS!

HARLEQUIN®

Blaze®

Red-hot reads!

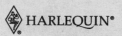

HARLEQUIN®

American ROMANCE®

A THREE-BOOK SERIES BY BELOVED AUTHOR

Judy Christenberry

Dallas Duets

What's behind the doors of
the Yellow Rose Lane apartments?
Love, Texas-style!

THE MARRYING KIND
May 2007

Jonathan Davis was many things—a millionaire,
a player, a catch. But he'd never be a husband.
For him, "marriage" equaled "mistake." Diane Black
was a forever kind of woman, a babies-and-minivan
kind of woman. But John was confident he could
date her and still avoid that trap.
Until he kissed her…

Also watch for:
DADDY NEXT DOOR
January 2007

MOMMY FOR A MINUTE
August 2007

Available wherever Harlequin books are sold.

www.eHarlequin.com

HARM07JC

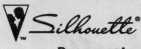

Silhouette®
Romantic
SUSPENSE

**Sparked by Danger,
Fueled by Passion.**

*This month and every month look for
four new heart-racing romances
set against a backdrop of suspense!*

Available in May 2007

Safety in Numbers
(Wild West Bodyguards miniseries)
by Carla Cassidy

Jackson's Woman
by Maggie Price

Shadow Warrior
(Night Guardians miniseries)
by Linda Conrad

One Cool Lawman
by Diane Pershing

Available wherever you buy books!

HARLEQUIN®

Blaze™

COMING NEXT MONTH

#321 BEYOND SEDUCTION Kathleen O'Reilly
The Red Choo Diaries, Bk. 3
The last thing respected talk-show host Sam Porter wants is to be the subject of a sex blog—but that's exactly what happens when up-and-coming writer Mercedes Brooks gets hold of him…and never wants to let him go!

#322 THE EX-GIRLFRIENDS' CLUB Rhonda Nelson
Ben Wilder is stunned when he discovers a Web site dedicated to bashing him. Sure, he's a little wild. So what? Then he learns Eden Rutherford, his first love, is behind the site, and decides some payback is in order. And he's going to start by showing Eden *exactly* what she's been missing….

#323 THE MAN TAMER Cindi Myers
It's All About Attitude…
Can't get your man to behave? Columnist Rachel Westover has the answer: man taming, aka behavior modification. Too bad she can't get Garret Kelly to obey. Sure, he's hers to command between the sheets, but outside…well, there might be something to be said for going wild!

#324 DOUBLE DARE Tawny Weber
Audra Walker is the ultimate bad girl. And to prove it, she takes a friend's dare—to hit on the next guy who comes through the door of the bar. Lucky for her, the guy's a definite hottie. Too bad he's also a cop….

#325 KISS AND DWELL Kelley St. John
The Sexth Sense, Bk. 1
Monique Vicknair has a secret—she and her family are mediums, charged with the job of helping lost souls cross over. But when Monique discovers her next assignment is sexy Ryan Chappelle, the last thing she wants to do is send him away. Because Ryan is way too much man to be a ghost….

#326 HOT FOR HIM Sarah Mayberry
Secret Lives of Daytime Divas, Bk. 3
Beating her rival for a coveted award has put Claudia Dostis on top. But when Leandro Mandalor challenges her to address the sizzle between them, her pride won't let her back down. In this battle for supremacy the gloves—and a lot of other clothes—are coming off!

www.eHarlequin.com

HBCNM0407